## MALLORY ON STRIKE

"Excuse me, everyone, but I've got an important announcement to make." My heart was pounding in my chest.

"Is it about Miss Frugal?" Claudia giggled, nudging Stacey in the ribs. Stacey swatted at her to stop, but she was grinning.

I closed my eyes and said the words really fast. "It's about me and the BSC. I would like to be demoted."

There was a dead silence. Finally Kristy spoke.

"You're kidding, aren't you?"

I opened my eyes and shook my head. "No."

Jessi, who was sitting next to me, grabbed my hand. "Mallory, that's silly." . . . .

"I don't know when I'll be able to take another job," I said, my voice getting tighter and louder. "So please demote me. If you don't, I'll resign!"

Scholastic Children's Books,
Scholastic Publications Ltd,
7–9 Pratt Street, London NW1 0AE

Scholastic Inc.,
730 Broadway, New York, NY 10003, USA

Scholastic Canada Ltd,
123 Newkirk Road, Richmond Hill,
Ontario L4C 3G5, Canada

Ashton Scholastic Pty Ltd,
P O Box 579, Gosford, New South Wales,
Australia

Ashton Scholastic Ltd,
Private Bag 1, Penrose, Auckland,
New Zealand

First published in the USA by Scholastic Inc., 1991
First published in the UK by Scholastic Publications Ltd, 1994

ISBN 0 590 55439 5

Typeset in Plantin by Contour Typesetters, Southall, London
Printed by Cox & Wyman Ltd, Reading, Berks.

10 9 8 7 6 5 4 3 2 1

# MALLORY ON STRIKE

## Ann M. Martin

Hippo

*Also in the Babysitters Club series:*

*Look out for:*
Jessi's Wish

*The author gratefully acknowledges
Jahnna Beecham
and
Malcolm Hillgartner
for their help in
preparing this manuscript.*

# 1st CHAPTER

Today—at exactly 2.15 PM—my whole life changed. That was when Mr Dougherty, my creative writing teacher, told my class about Young Authors Day.

I'm Mallory Pike. Most people call me Mal. I'm eleven years old, and I want to be a writer. Correction. I am *going* to be a writer. And I am going to write about everything. And illustrate my books, too.

Anyway, Mr Dougherty announced the event to my creative writing class, which is a special one that I was invited to join because of my writing talent. (Does that sound too conceited? I hope not.) I was *so* thrilled when I was picked for his class because not only is Mr Dougherty the coolest, funniest, cleverest teacher I have ever had, but he has actually had a book *published*. He's a real author like I want to be. The kids in my class call him Mr D. He seems to like it, too. He's

1

sort of round and jolly, with a big, bushy moustache that he twirls around his finger whenever he's pleased with something. He always twirls it when we call him Mr D.

Now, where was I? Oh, right. Young Authors Day. Mr D. told us that it is a special day celebrating future writers. A famous author is going to talk to the whole school about writing and how to get a book published, and then a contest is going to be held, with prizes going to the best writers in Stoneybrook Middle School. There are lots of categories that we can enter: Best Poem, Best Short Story, Best Mystery, Best Illustration of a Story, and (the one I hope to win) Best Overall Fiction for the Sixth Grade. When I told Mr D. that was the category I wanted to enter, his eyes twinkled and he twirled the ends of his moustache. (So I know he was pleased.)

I couldn't wait to tell Jessi about it. She's my best friend. Jessica Ramsey is her full name, but no one ever calls her that, except maybe her parents when they're cross with her. Jessi is beautiful. She's tall and thin, with wonderful long legs that are just right for a ballerina, which is what she is. And not just any ballerina, either, but one of the best at this really good ballet school she goes to in Stamford. Just to show you how great a dancer she is, Jessi's had the lead role in several major productions recently, including *Coppélia*, in which she played Swanilda.

I go to every one of her performances, and so do the rest of my friends in the Baby-sitters Club—but I'll tell you about them later.

Jessi is the same age as me, eleven. We're both junior officers in the BSC (Babysitters Club). We're a lot alike except for a few things. First, I come from a huge family with eight kids. And guess what? Three of them are identical triplets. But even though they look alike, Byron, Jordan, and Adam have very different personalities—especially Byron, who's quieter and more sensitive than his brothers.

People often say we're staircase kids, which means that we were born one after the other. And they're right. You see, I'm the eldest. The triplets, who are ten, are right behind me. My sister Vanessa is nine, Nicky is eight, Margo is seven, and last but not least is Claire. She's five. Can you imagine eating dinner with that many people every night? It can be a zoo, some-times. But Mum and Dad don't seem to be bothered by it. They're great.

Everyone in my family has chestnut brown hair and blue eyes. And out of all ten of us, Nicky and I are the ones who wear glasses. Which I hate. I've begged my parents for contact lenses, but they say I have to wait until I'm older. I also wear a brace. (The clear plastic kind.) And while we're on the subject of things I hate, let's talk about my nose. I got it from my grandfather. If I could get rid of it, I would.

Jessi doesn't wear a brace or glasses, and her family is normal-sized (two parents and three kids, plus her Aunt Cecelia). Jessi's eight-year-old sister is named Becca (short for Rebecca), and her baby brother is nicknamed Squirt. His real name is John Philip Ramsey, Jr., which is a very big name for such a little person.

Another difference between Jessi and me is that she's black and I'm white. In fact, Jessi is the only black pupil in the whole of the sixth grade. It doesn't mean anything to me, but it did to a lot of people when the Ramseys first moved to Stoneybrook, Connecticut. (That's where we live.) I'm ashamed to say that some of the people in Stoneybrook were pretty rotten to them at first. But things have got much better for the Ramseys.

I told Jessi my news about Young Authors Day and the writing contest as we headed home after school. Since it was Friday, we were feeling pretty great. When I told her that I had a chance at winning the Best Overall Fiction award for the whole sixth grade, Jessi gave me a hug. The two of us stood on the street corner, where we usually go our separate ways, squealing with excitement. We didn't even care that Justin Forbes and Howie Johnson, two eighth-graders, heard us. I was too happy to be embarrassed. And Jessi, my best friend, was happy for me.

"Just think!" I said, pushing my glasses up on my nose. "I've got the whole weekend to work on my prize-winning short story."

"Do you have any idea what you're going to write about?" Jessi asked.

I shook my head. "I'm planning to hole up in my room and use the next two days to come up with the perfect award-winning idea."

"You could write a horse story," Jessi suggested. "Everyone loves them, especially the ones by—"

"Marguerite Henry!" we both said at the same time. She's our favourite author.

"I'm going to have to check my journal," I said after we stopped giggling. (I'm not sure why we were giggling so much. Maybe just because it was Friday and we were happy.) "I've written a lot of ideas in there. I think I'll take a look at it and then decide."

I keep my journal under my mattress in my bedroom, which I share with Vanessa. Not that I need to hide it from her. She's a poet and understands a writer's need for privacy.

"First I'm going to finish all my homework this afternoon, so I can give my complete attention to my story." Then I groaned when I realized my homework was mostly maths and science, my two hardest subjects. That was going to take *a lot* of concentration, which was hard because I was feeling so excited.

Jessi checked the little gold watch she was wearing and reminded me, "You'd better get started on your homework right away. We have a BSC meeting in exactly two hours."

"Two hours? Yikes!" I waved goodbye to Jessi and shouted, "See you at Claud's!" (Claudia Kishi is the vice-chairman of the BSC, and we hold our meetings at her house.)

Then I hurried home. Our house is medium-sized for such a big family. In fact, sometimes it seems tiny. My brothers, Nicky and the triplets, have one bedroom (two sets of bunk beds); my two youngest sisters, Claire and Margo, share another; and Vanessa and I share a third. My parents have the master bedroom. You can imagine with that many people in such a small space, something's always happening. Today was no exception.

I opened the front door and was about to hang my jacket in the hall cupboard when Claire wrapped her arms around my legs and shrieked, "The bogeymen are after me!"

"Bogey*men*?" I repeated. (Usually there is only one bogeyman, and he

6

lives in a cupboard. Everybody knows that.)

Claire pointed to the living room, where the triplets were crouched like cats ready to pounce. Byron was wearing a catcher's mask; Adam was wearing a diving mask, with big flippers on his feet; and Jordan was carrying Dad's tennis racquet in his hand, a ski mask pulled over his face. At first glance they really were quite scary.

"Moozie is gone," Claire cried, her lower lip quivering. (That's what Claire sometimes calls Mum—Moozie.) "They napped her."

"Napped?" I repeated. "You mean, kidnapped?"

Claire let out a sob. "Yes."

The three boys ignored her cry and leaped up on the sofa with a loud growl.

"Now, stop that!" I ordered. "You're scaring Claire."

"We're not trying to," Jordan said, lowering his tennis racquet. He looked disappointed. "We're just playing Mutant Invaders from Outer Space."

"Well, play outside," I said, gesturing towards the backgarden. "I have to finish my homework, and I'm going to need complete quiet."

"She's no fun," Byron mumbled, as he led Adam and Jordan through the hall and into the kitchen. "Let's go and see if any other invaders have landed."

After the boys had gone, I made a move for the stairs but forgot that Claire was still holding onto my knees. "Claire, you can let go, now," I said, prising open her fingers. "The bogeymen have gone. Where's Mum?"

"I told you," Claire murmured, rubbing her eyes with her fists. "They napped her."

"Where'd they take her?"

Claire pointed up, so I took her by the hand and led her to the foot of the stairs. "Let's see if we can find her."

As we climbed the carpeted stairs, I checked the clock on the mantelpiece in the living room. Fifteen minutes had already passed since I'd left Jessi on the corner, and I'd barely got through the front door. That meant I was going to have to work *really* fast on my homework.

We peeped into my parents' room. Margo was sitting at my mother's dressing table. Two bright blue stripes were painted over her eyes, two red circles on her cheeks, and her lips were smeared with orange lipstick.

Claire saw Margo and clapped her hands. "Look how pretty she is! I want to do that!"

"Oh, no, you don't!" I said. "I don't think Mummy would like you to use her make-up. In fact," I added for Margo's benefit, "she's not going to be very happy when she sees what Margo's done to her face."

Margo smiled at her reflection. "It's all right. Mum said I could."

"She did?" Mum is usually pretty easygoing, but when it comes to *big* messes, she draws the line. As a precautionary measure I said, "Margo, you look really pretty, but I think you should put the make-up away now."

Then I led Claire to my bedroom, aware that the minutes were ticking away. I found Vanessa lying on her bed, holding a flowered journal in one hand and her lavender pen in the other. She had that dreamy look she always gets when she's working on a poem.

"Vanessa, I need your help!" I pleaded. "Could you take Claire for me? Mum seems to have disappeared, Margo has just painted her face with make-up, and the triplets are in the back garden, looking like a weird ad for *Sports Illustrated*."

Vanessa blinked her big blue eyes at me. "Hmmm?" she asked.

"Earth to Vanessa!" I said, waving my hand in front of her face. "Take Claire. And find Mum."

Vanessa seemed to tune in this time and got off her bed. "Where *is* Mum?"

I rolled my eyes at the ceiling. My sister is very bright, but she can be a real airhead. "If I knew where she was," I replied, "I wouldn't be asking you to find her. But she's probably around here somewhere."

That seemed to be good enough for Vanessa. She obediently took Claire's hand and went off in search of our mother.

"At last!" I said, shutting the door after them. I flopped down on my bed, fluffed up two pillows behind my back, dug into my book bag (which I had been lugging all over the house with me), and opened my maths book to page ninety-eight. I took a piece of paper and a pencil out of my bag and sighed. "Peace and quiet."

I spoke too soon. The door flew open and banged against the wall. It was Nicky, and he was holding his finger.

"Frodo bit me!" he cried, running up to the edge of the bed. Frodo's our hamster.

"What?" I closed my maths book. "Let me see."

Nicky held out his finger to show me the bite. It was the same finger he had once broken playing volleyball. It was slightly crooked but other than that, nothing was there. No blood, no hamster teeth marks, nothing. But I'd done enough babysitting to know that when a kid is upset, it doesn't matter if the bite is real or imagined. It's real to the child. I got off the bed and said, "Nicky, that must really hurt."

"It does," Nicky said, clutching his wrist.

"Why did Frodo bite you?" I asked.

"I don't know." Nicky puffed out his lower lip. "I was being really good to him. I was sharing my bar of chocolate with him and he wouldn't let go of it. When I tried to take it back, he bit me. And then he ran away."

I ran for the door. "Frodo's loose?"

Nicky nodded. I put my hands to my head. It was starting to ache. "Come on," I said. "Let's go and find him."

I spent the next half hour on my knees, searching for a little furry hamster. Every time I'd almost catch him, behind a shoe in the wardrobe or under the boys' bunk beds, Nicky would shout, "I'll get him!" and Frodo would dart across the floor to another hiding place. We finally managed to nab him when Frodo ran straight into Nicky's book bag.

By the end of that episode, my head was really starting to throb. I had just settled onto my bed again when a voice shouted from downstairs, "Mallory! Mal, darling, are you upstairs?"

It was Mum. And she was calling me darling. She probably wanted me to do something for her.

"Mal, the boys are having some sort of argument in the back garden. Would you deal with it for me? I've just seen Margo and Claire in the kitchen. I told Margo she could play with my Chapstick, and she thought that meant *all* of my make-up."

"I know." I groaned as I got off the bed and walked to the top of the stairs. I rubbed my temples with my fingers while Mum listed the series of disasters that had happened in the last thirty minutes.

"Claire got some silly idea that I had been kidnapped, when all I told her was that I wanted to take a little nap later this afternoon. Then, while I was down in the basement getting some tins of tomatoes for dinner, the boys tried to frighten her."

"I'm telling!" Jordan bellowed from the back garden. "You're going to get it!"

"No, *you* are!" Adam replied.

"Are not!"

"Are too!"

A loud crash sounded from the kitchen, and my mother put her hands to her face. "My casserole!" She looked up at me and pleaded, "Mallory, please do something about the boys!"

I wanted to tell Mum the great news about Young Authors Day, and how I planned to win the contest. I also wanted to tell her that if my sisters and brothers didn't leave me alone, I'd never finish my homework and then I'd never get a chance to start my story. But my mum looked worse than I felt, so I held my tongue.

I checked the mantelpiece clock again as I came downstairs and saw that it was nearly 5:15. I had just enough time to quieten the triplets and get over to Claudia's house.

So I opened the back door—and the triplets ploughed right into me. Then Nicky ran up behind me, shouting, "Mallory! Frodo's escaped again!"

I felt this tight lump forming in my throat, and suddenly I wanted to cry. Seven brothers and sisters is just too many! I hate to admit this but sometimes I wish they would disappear so that I could have a normal life. Like Jessi and the rest of my friends . . .

# 2nd CHAPTER

At 5:20 I grabbed my bike and cycled as fast as I could away from my four brothers, my three sisters, and my unfinished homework. I ducked my head down low and made a beeline for Bradford Court, where Friday's meeting of the Babysitters Club was about to start. I suppose now would be the best time to tell you about the members of the BSC, since the Club is one of the most important things in my life (along with Young Authors Day now).

Kristy Thomas is our chairman. She's really energetic and has a lot of great ideas. The best one, of course, was dreaming up the Babysitters Club. Kristy has brown hair and brown eyes, is the shortest girl in the eighth grade, and doesn't care much about clothes. She usually wears jeans, trainers, a polo-neck, and a sweater, and she doesn't need a bra yet. She can usually be found wearing an old baseball cap with a picture of a collie on it.

Kristy loves sports. In fact, the walls of her bedroom are covered with posters of gymnasts and football players and even a few Olympic posters. I suppose you can tell that she's pretty much of a tomboy. Kristy's also got a big mouth, which sometimes gets her into trouble, and she can be pretty bossy at times. But she's a lot of fun, and she's terrific with kids. In fact, she coaches a softball team called Kristy's Krushers. The Krushers sometimes play Bart's Bashers, who are coached by none other than (the extremely cute) Bart Taylor. He's sort of Kristy's boyfriend and lives in her neighbourhood but goes to a private school. (All the main BSC members go to Stoneybrook Middle School.)

My family, which at this moment is driving me crazy, is huge and so is Kristy's. But her family is all mixed up like a crazy quilt. (You know those quilts that are made of funny shapes and colours pieced together with no real design?) She has two older brothers at high school called Sam and Charlie. Then there's David Michael, who's much younger. He's seven.

Just after David Michael was born, Kristy's father walked out on the family, leaving Mrs Thomas with four kids. Then guess what? Mrs Thomas met Watson Brewer—a genuine millionaire! They got married, and the whole family moved from their smallish house (Kristy used to live on Bradford Court opposite Claud) to Watson's mansion on the other side of town.

Now here's where things become mixed up like a crazy quilt. Watson has two little kids from his first marriage, Karen and Andrew, who are seven and four. They stay with the Brewers every other weekend, and Kristy adores them. But *then* Kristy's mum and Watson adopted Emily Michelle, a Vietnamese girl. She's two and a half. And since the family was getting so big, Nannie, Kristy's grandmother, moved in to help run the house and look after Emily. (Nannie is not what you'd imagine—prim and proper like some old ladies. She wears jeans and goes bowling.) So when everyone is there, the house is pretty full.

Claudia Kishi is, as I told you before, the BSC's vice-chairman. Claud is artistic, ultra-trendy, and gorgeous. She's Japanese-American and has these beautiful almond-shaped eyes and shiny black hair that is *soooooo* long and straight. She wears it a million different ways: a French plait down her back, double and triple French plaits with sparkly ribbons woven into them, or sometimes just pulled up on one side with a wide hairslide that she made herself. She makes her own jewellery out of clay or papier-mâché. Sometimes she'll wear a pink flamingo in one ear with a palm tree in the other, and then put a tiny gold monkey on top of the palm tree. (She has two holes pierced in one ear.) Claudia can wear anything and it looks great. Like she'll wear polka dot leggings with a short red skirt. Then she'll wear a long-sleeved T-shirt with a black waistcoat (covered with cool pins that she's made herself) over that. Sometimes she decides to go fifties and wears penny loafers with white ankle socks.

Claudia may be cool, but she's a pretty lousy pupil. Her teachers say it's because she doesn't try hard enough. It doesn't help that her sister, Janine, is a certified genius. (I'm not kidding. She has an IQ of 196!) Janine is sixteen years old and already goes to classes at Stoneybrook University. While Janine spends most of her time at her computer, Claudia keeps busy working on her art, reading Nancy Drew mysteries (which she hides from her parents because they think she should be reading *important* books), and eating junk food. She's crazy about junk food and hides snacks all over her room: Maltesers in her chest of drawers, M&M's in her jewellery box, jelly beans and Hula Hoops in her shoes. With all of those sweets, she's never had bad skin in her life. It's not fair!

Anyway, Claud lives with her parents and her sister and, until recently, her beloved grandmother, Mimi. Mimi died a while ago, and this was hard on Claud and the rest of us. We adored Mimi and miss her very much.

Luckily for Claud, her best friend and the BSC's treasurer, Stacey McGill, is back in Stoneybrook for good. (We hope.) Stacey was one of the original four members of the BSC, and she used to live in the house where Jessi lives. (Now Stacey lives in the house right behind me!) Recently her dad got transferred back to New York City (where Stacey was born and grew up) and then something went wrong between her parents. They ended up getting a divorce, and Stacey and her mum moved back to Stoneybrook. So Stacey spends holidays and certain weekends in New York City with her father. She's very sophisticated and wears wild clothes and Claudia's homemade earrings (everyone in the BSC has pierced ears except Kristy and Mary Anne). She has clear blue eyes and her blonde hair is usually permed and always in the absolute trendiest style.

Stacey has one big problem (besides her parents' divorce). She's got diabetes. That means that her body can't process sugar, so she has to stay on a very strict diet. She can't eat sweets, except for controlled amounts of fruits, and she has to give herself (are you ready for this?) injections of insulin. EVERY DAY. I couldn't do it. No way! I hate injections. But Stacey has to. If she's not extremely careful she could go into a diabetic coma. (Not long ago, she got really ill when she wasn't eating properly and her blood sugar went haywire. She had to be put in the hospital in New York.) But Stacey is a strong person and manages to cope pretty well.

Mary Anne Spier is the club's secretary, and she's also Kristy's best friend. They grew up together, and they even look a little bit alike. They're both short, with brown hair and brown eyes. But they are also very different. Mary Anne is quiet and extremely romantic. She's a good listener and is very sensitive (actually, she cries a lot). Mary Anne was an only child until her dad recently married Dawn Schafer's mum (which I'll tell you about in a minute). Mary Anne's mum died when Mary Anne was really young, and Mr Spier had to bring her up all by himself. I suppose that's what made him so strict. He hardly let her do anything, or go anywhere. He even told her what she could and couldn't wear.

For a while, Mary Anne dressed like a first-grader, and it really embarrassed her. But then things changed. Mary Anne finally proved to her father that she had grown up, and he let her choose her own clothes (which are much trendier now). Then she met cute Logan Bruno and they started going out together. (Mary Anne is the only member of the BSC to have a steady boyfriend!) She and Logan have had some problems, but they seem to have worked things out, and we're happy that's so. Logan, who's from Kentucky and speaks with this really great drawl, is an associate member of the BSC. That means he doesn't attend meetings. (That's okay with me. Even though I like him, it's nice not having boys at club meetings.) But he can be called on to babysit in an emergency. Shannon Kilbourne, a friend of Kristy's, is also an associate member.

Mary Anne's other best friend (and stepsister) is Dawn Schafer. Dawn is the BSC's alternate officer, which means if a club member gets ill or is away, she can take over that person's position. It's a big responsibility, but Dawn can handle it. She has a lot of self-confidence.

Dawn is absolutely gorgeous. She has this L-O-N-G blonde hair that is almost white from being in the California sun (which is where she's from—southern California). She has blue eyes and is a very individual dresser. I mean, Dawn wears whatever she wants: three different coloured T-shirts at once with lots of necklaces (plus she has two holes pierced in each ear) and a short denim skirt. Her style is trendy but casual.

Dawn wouldn't be caught dead with a Twix or a hamburger in her hand. She's a real health food nut. You know, rice and beans and pulses and that kind of stuff.

Mrs Schafer moved Dawn and her

brother, Jeff, to Connecticut about a year ago, after Dawn's parents got divorced. (Mrs Schafer had grown up in Stoneybrook. Soon after they got here, Dawn and Jeff were both homesick for California and really missed their father. Also, Jeff was having a hard time at school, so he moved back with his father, which split the Schafer family in two.)

Then this really weird (I mean, *extremely* weird) thing happened. First, Dawn and Mary Anne became best friends. *Then* they found out that Mary Anne's dad and Dawn's mum went out together when they were at high school. So Dawn and Mary Anne arranged for them to re-meet and guess what? They instantly fell in love again. After what seemed like an endless amount of time, they finally got married, and the Spiers and Mary Anne's kitten, Tigger, moved into the Schafers' big old farmhouse. I know that sometimes Dawn really misses her dad and brother and California (let's face it, she's been through a lot of changes), but she seems to cope really well. Besides, now that she's got a stepfather as well as a stepsister who, as I said, just happens to be her best friend, I think she's much happier.

My best friend, Jessi, whom I've already told you about, and I are the junior officers of the BSC. That's because we're the youngest members and can only babysit after school and at weekends.

I was so busy thinking about the Club and my unfinished homework and Young Authors Day that I didn't even notice the red-and-white-striped ball that rolled across the street in front of me.

"Look out!" a small boy in a cowboy shirt and hat shouted. I swerved to miss the ball, and my front tyre bumped against the kerb directly in front of Claudia's house. Luckily, I didn't fall, but I was embarrassed that that little kid had seen me almost crash like that. I steadied myself, then wheeled my bike up the Kishis' drive.

# 3rd
# CHAPTER

I opened the Kishis' front door and raced upstairs to Claudia's room. The rest of the club members were already there, waiting in their usual spots. Kristy was sitting in the director's chair, wearing her visor and a pencil tucked over one ear. The club notebook was lying open on her lap. Claudia, Mary Anne, and Dawn were lined up on Claud's bed, their backs leaning against the wall. Stacey was straddling Claud's desk chair, her arms draped over the top rung of the back. I took my place on the floor next to Jessi just as Claudia's digital alarm clock changed from 5:29 to 5:30.

All club meetings start on time and last exactly thirty minutes. We meet three times a week on Monday, Wednesday, and Friday afternoons. Parents know that and phone us during meetings to arrange sitters. But

23

I'm getting ahead of myself. First, let me tell you how this fantastic idea got started.

It all began when Kristy, Claudia, Stacey, and Mary Anne were in the seventh grade at Stoneybrook Middle School. I was a lowly fifth-grader at Stoneybrook Elementary, and Jessi and Dawn hadn't even moved here yet.

Back then, Kristy, Claud, and Mary Anne liked to babysit, but they always set up jobs on their own. Then one day Mrs Thomas needed someone to look after Kristy's six-year-old brother, David Michael. Kristy and her brothers Sam and Charlie were busy, so Mrs Thomas spent practically forever on the telephone trying to arrange a sitter. It was while Kristy was watching her mother make all those phone calls that the brilliant idea hit her. Wouldn't it be wonderful, she thought, if parents could make one phone call and reach a lot of sitters?

Kristy immediately invited Mary Anne and Claudia to form a babysitters club with her. Then the girls decided they needed four members, so Claudia suggested they invite Stacey to join. And that was the start of the BSC.

Claudia's room was the logical head-quarters for the club, mainly because she's got her own private telephone line. (I told you she was cool.) And the girls worked out that, since they would be spending a lot of time in Claud's room, she should be made vice-chairman. So she was.

Then the club members advertised their business by placing an announcement in the *Stoneybrook News* and passing out leaflets, and they got calls at their very first meeting. (One person needed a dog-sitter, but that's another story.) Anyway, soon business was booming. So when Dawn Schafer moved to town and became friends with Mary Anne, the girls asked her to join the club, and she became the alternate officer. Then Stacey moved back to New York City, and the club members asked Jessi and me to join as junior officers. Of course, when Stacey returned to Stoneybrook, we let her straight back into the club. And since she really likes numbers, and Dawn isn't that crazy about them, Stacey became the official treasurer once again (Dawn had taken over for her while she was away).

There are now seven members of the club. I have to tell you that during BSC meetings, Claud's bedroom feels pretty crowded. And when we're all talking or giggling (which we do quite a bit of), it sounds like a major party is going on.

Of course, Kristy tries to keep things from getting too out of hand. In fact, she is very business-like at our meetings. She makes sure they start promptly at 5:30, and she's not very happy about anyone being late. Kristy also makes sure we keep the club notebook up-to-date.

What's the club notebook? It's like a diary. We're supposed to write up every job in the notebook. That way the other members can find out if one kid is afraid of the dark and needs a night-light left on, or if another kid is having trouble with school and needs help. It can be really useful in solving problems. It also helps us know which kids are going to be *pains*. (Like the Arnold twins, who actually turned out to be nice. The notebook certainly helped me with them.) I don't mind writing in the notebook, and neither does Kristy, but no one else is too keen on it, especially Claudia (maybe because she's such a poor speller). Also, we're supposed to read the notebook once a week, to keep up with things.

The Kid-Kits were another great Kristy idea. She suggested that we each get a cardboard box, decorate it, then fill it with toys and fun things for kids to play with. Mine is packed with books (of course), games and other old toys of mine, crayons, colouring books, stickers, scissors, and glue. I often take my Kid-Kit with me when I baby-sit. Children love it. Kid-kits are also good for business, because when kids are happy, their parents are happy, and then they call the BSC and give us more jobs!

Mary Anne has the hardest job. As the BSC secretary, she's in charge of the club record book (another one of Kristy's great ideas). She writes down the addresses of all our clients, their phone numbers, and the rates they pay. More importantly, Mary Anne assigns every single job. That means she has to know all of our schedules. Like, when Jessi takes her ballet lessons, or Stacey's got a doctor's appointment, or when I have to go to the (Ugh!) orthodontist, or when Kristy's Krushers have a practice. Even so, I don't think Mary Anne has ever made a mistake.

As club treasurer, Stacey collects subs from us every Monday. We grumble about paying them, but that's just because it's hard to part with money. Stacey keeps a record of the money in the treasury, then doles it out to pay for Claudia's phone bill and Kristy's lift to the meetings (we pay her brother Charlie to drive her across town in his car). Our subs also go for replacing items (like crayons and colouring books) in our Kid-Kits, and planning and buying snacks for fun BSC activities like pizza parties or slumber parties. Stacey certainly loves collecting our money, too. She gets this wicked gleam in her eye whenever she pats the manila envelope holding our subs.

So that's how the club works. Three times a week we gather at Claudia's and wait for the phone to ring. Which today it did immediately. Stacey, who was closest, called out, "I'll get it!" She reached for the phone. "Hello, Babysitters Club," she said. "Oh, hi, Mrs Prezzioso."

The Prezziosos live on Burnt Hill Road and are friends of my family. They're a little prim and proper but nice. They have two daughters—Jenny, who's four, and a baby, Andrea. The Prezziosos needed a sitter for the following Saturday afternoon, so Mary Anne, who likes Jenny a lot, volunteered. As soon as Stacey hung up, the phone rang again. And then it rang again. And again.

"That's four sitters for Saturday," Mary Anne commented as she assigned the Papadakises to Kristy and the Arnold twins to Jessi.

Dawn, who'd just agreed to sit for Jamie and Lucy Newton, nodded. "Something really big must be happening."

Claudia was busy searching through her desk drawers for a bag of crisps she had hidden the night before. "Didn't you know?" she said. "Chez Maurice is serving a special luncheon. They're going to donate half the money they make to the Stoneybrook Public Library." She found the crisps in a pile of dirty clothes, tore open the bag, and took a loud, crunchy bite of one. "Chez Maurice has the most dibble food." (Dibble is a word we made up that means

28

incredible.) "It's my parents' favourite restaurant."

Claud passed the crisps round the room and even Dawn, who as I told you is a major health food nut, took a handful. I suppose listening to Claudia describe all the delicious French dishes at Chez Maurice made everyone hungry. Everyone except me.

Too many thoughts were churning in my head to pay much attention. Young Authors Day was only four weeks away. A month isn't much time when you are trying to write an award-winning story. I mean, I've sometimes spent as long as two months working on a short poem. I wanted to give this story one hundred per cent of my effort for two reasons: 1) I wanted to win the award for Best Overall Fiction for the Sixth Grade (that would mean that I *do* have talent, and might really become a famous author one day), and 2) I wanted to make my wonderful teacher, Mr Dougherty, proud of me.

"Then there's this delicious dish called *anguilles rotis*," Claudia said, as she shoved another handful of crisps into her mouth and flopped back on her bed. "It tastes all buttery and garlicky" is what she said, but what everyone heard was, "Uf tasel buddery an gawikee."

Jessi, who is very good with languages and is studying French (mainly because that's the language of ballet), shot Claudia a funny look. "Did you say *anguilles*?" (Jessi pronounced it "On-guiy.")

Claudia nodded.

Jessi wrinkled her nose. "That's French for eels!"

"*Eels!*" Claud nearly spat out her crisps onto her tie-dyed T-shirt. "Oh, gross!" She leaped off the bed and hopped in a circle, saying, "Ugh! Ugh! Ugh!"

The rest of us howled with laughter as we watched her dance around in disgust. I was still worrying about my homework, and my story, and when I was ever going to get a chance to work on them. Jessi must have noticed I'd stopped laughing before anyone else because she tapped me on the shoulder and said, "Can you believe it? Claud ate eels and didn't even know it."

Before I could respond, the phone rang again. Kristy, who was laughing just as loudly as the others, waved her arm for everyone to settle down. Then she put on a very serious face and picked up the phone.

"Babysitters Club," she said. "No job is too small. We'll give it our all!"

That made everyone burst out laughing again. But Mary Anne gestured for us to keep silent while Kristy listened intently, then nodded her head several times.

"I'll call you straight back, okay?" Kristy

hung up the phone and said, "That was Mrs Hobart. She needs a sitter for James, Mathew, and Johnny. Naturally, it's for Saturday. But Mrs Hobart isn't going to Chez Maurice."

"To eat eels," Stacey whispered, giving Claudia a nudge. Claud aimed her finger down her throat, and that set Dawn to giggling.

Kristy adjusted her visor and tried to look like a stern chairman. "Mrs Hobart is taking a class and needs someone to sit with the boys for *four* Saturdays, starting tomorrow. She's willing to pay extra if the sitter will help them with their homework." By the way, there are four Hobart boys. The oldest is Ben. He's my age, and sometimes we go to dances and stuff together. I supposed Ben had said he would watch his brothers but had had to back out at the last minute.

Mary Anne checked the club notebook and shook her head. "Boy, we're really filled up on Saturday. We just booked four of us today, and Claudia and Stacey already have jobs. It looks like Mallory's the only one who can do it."

Kristy turned and smiled at me. "Lucky you. You'll be able to earn a lot of money on this one."

I thought it over quickly. If I sat for the Hobarts on Saturdays, that would leave me only one day each weekend to work on my story, finish my homework, and do my chores. That just wasn't enough time. It was a tough decision, but I had to make it.

"I'm sorry, Mary Anne," I said, "but I'll have to turn this one down."

Everyone stared at me in surprise. "Do you have another sitting job?" Stacey asked.

I shook my head. "No. I just would rather not take this one, if that's okay."

I was about to tell the club about Young Authors Day, and how important the contest was to me, but the looks on their faces made me stop. I was afraid they'd think I was being selfish. I pursed my lips and stared at my hands in my lap, hoping they'd stop staring at me.

"Well . . ." Mary Anne shrugged. Her voice trailed off as she studied the notebook. "I suppose we'll just have to call on one of our associate members."

Kristy picked up the phone. "I'll phone Shannon Kilbourne. She told me she needed some work."

I hardly looked up during the rest of the meeting. I was too embarrassed. Luckily it lasted only a few more minutes. At six o'clock, when Kristy announced that the meeting of the BSC was officially adjourned, I hurried out of the Kishi house and grabbed my bike. I didn't even wait to talk to Jessi. My feelings were too jumbled up. I needed time to think.

# 4th CHAPTER

I set my alarm for seven o'clock the next morning. Believe me, it was agony getting up so early. Usually I try to sleep at least until eight on Saturdays. Vanessa was still in bed, so I got dressed as quietly as I could and tiptoed down to the TV room on the bottom floor of our house. I'd made up my mind to finish my homework early. Then I would have the rest of the day to work on my award-winning story.

It was weird to hear so much quiet. Usually our house is filled with noise, but the only sound I heard as I worked on my maths problems was Mum in the kitchen above me. I listened to her grind the coffee beans and fill the coffee maker. Then I heard her slippers shuffle across the lino-leum to the fridge. Since it was Saturday, I guessed she was whipping up pancake batter for breakfast. It's a Pike family favourite. Sometimes for a treat she puts chocolate chips in the pancakes.

After I got used to the quiet, I focused all my attention on my homework. It was amazing. I finished the maths problems in less than an hour and hurried on to my science. By then, the house was starting to sound like itself again.

I heard the triplets clatter down the stairs and turn on the stereo in the living room. Shortly after that I heard Nicky leap down the stairs to join them. They had their usual Saturday morning argument over which station to listen to. Finally I heard my father's voice say, "Truce! Now, we'll decide this fairly and squarely." Fairly and squarely meant Dad was going to flip a coin. There was silence, then Dad said, "Call!" and shortly after that, Nicky's voice shouted, "I won! I won!"

I could just imagine him hopping up and down, grinning wickedly over his victory. I hummed to myself as I worked on my final assignment. It was a book report for Mr Williams' English class. I had read the final chapter the night before, so the story was still fresh in my mind.

Just as I closed my notebook and put the cap back on my pen, my father called me from the kitchen.

"Mallory! Are you in the TV room?" Dad shouted. "Breakfast!"

I stretched my arms and arched my back.

I had been working solidly for two and a half hours, and the rumble in my stomach made me realize that I was starving.

"Be right there, Dad!"

I have to admit it, I felt great. I'd finished my homework, and now I was going to devote the rest of the day to being an authoress.

I took a deep breath when I reached the top of the steps. The house smelled of frying bacon, which is one of my favourite foods, and I hurried to the kitchen table.

"Where've you been, Mallory?" my mother asked as she put a plate of pancakes in the middle of the table. "I haven't seen you all morning."

"I finally finished my homework!" I flashed everyone my biggest smile and slid into a spot between Claire and Margo. From the look of their clothes, they had already been in the back garden, making mud pies.

"Good for you!" my mother said. "Then you won't mind taking Claire and Margo into the bathroom and washing their hands. They're a mess."

Claire gave me a toothy grin. "I made mud pie surprise."

"What was the surprise?" Vanessa asked, coming into the kitchen. She tried to stifle a yawn as she slumped onto a seat at the table. The back of her hair was tangled in a big knot that stood up like a bird's nest.

"Walnuts," Claire and Margo called back as I ushered them into the bathroom.

"Where did you get the nuts from?" I asked, grabbing a flannel and running some water on it.

"The walnuts were really stones, but we pretended we were making a chocolate walnut pie," Margo explained. The girls squeezed their eyes shut as I first cleaned their faces, then wiped their hands.

"Sounds delicious," I said, trying not to laugh. It actually *did* sound good. Not the stones and mud part but the chocolate with nuts. It made me hungry just thinking about it. I quickly dried their faces with a towel, and we hurried back to the table.

The second I sat down, Byron knocked over his milk, reaching for the syrup.

"Uh-oh," he said solemnly, as it ran all over the table.

"Mallory, darling," my mum called. "Would you see to that? I'm helping Jordan get these knots out of his shoelaces." She looked directly at Nicky. "*Somebody* tied his shoes together."

I leaped out of my chair once more and grabbed a sponge. With eight kids, you can imagine that spilled glasses of milk are a daily occurrence in our house. Usually it is pretty irritating. But today, because it was only ten o'clock and I had already finished my homework, I didn't mind.

It wasn't until after breakfast that things started to get out of control. I helped load the dishwasher and then followed Vanessa up to our room. Once inside, I shut the door and faced my sister, who was busily pulling on a pair of jeans and a T-shirt.

"Vanessa?"

"What?" she said without looking up.

"I'm working on a very important story for my creative writing class."

"Oh," Vanessa answered. "What's it about?"

"I'm not sure yet. I have to plan it first. But I need *absolute* privacy to work on it."

My sister just stared at me. Finally I spelled it out for her.

"Which means I'm going to need our bedroom all to myself today. So . . . would you mind staying out?"

Vanessa scrunched her eyebrows together in thought. She was obviously considering my request. "For how long?" she finally asked.

"All day. Or at least until I've stopped working."

Vanessa's eyebrows were still pressed together, which meant that she wasn't too keen about not being able to come into her own room. Thinking quickly, I added, "I'll give you a quarter."

After a few more seconds of thought, she nodded. "It's a deal. But you have to pay me now."

I thought she must want to buy something, so I didn't mind handing over the money in advance. I opened the drawer of my bedside table and reached into a little tin decorated with horses, where I keep some of my babysitting earnings. I pulled out a shiny quarter and placed it in her palm.

"Don't forget," I reminded her, "you have to stay out until I've finished working."

"I'll remember," Vanessa said, dropping the coin into her purse. Then she scooped up a few books and left the room.

I leaned two pillows against my headboard and sat up on the bed with my notebook in my lap. As I took the cap off my favourite pen, I sighed. "It's going to be a perfect day," I thought.

Boy, I couldn't have been more wrong! Not five minutes after Vanessa had left, a knock sounded on the door.

"Not fair, Vanessa!" I complained. "You promised."

"It's not Vanessa." My mother opened the door and stuck her head into the room. "It's me. I have a tiny favour to ask."

Tiny was an understatement.

"I saw an ad in the paper for a used lawn mower at this garage sale," my mother continued, "and your father and I want to drive over and take a took at it. The triplets are coming with us. Would you watch the other kids for thirty minutes?"

My pen hadn't even touched the page and already I had to stop working. "Okay." I shut my notebook reluctantly and went downstairs to babysit.

At least my parents were true to their word. They were back in half an hour. But before I could return to my story, another knock sounded on my door. This time it was my father.

"Mal? May I talk to you for a second?"

"Sure, Dad," I said, trying not to sound too irritated.

"Listen, I'm going to help Margo and the boys set up the badminton net in the back garden," he said. "Would you mind making Claire a PBJ?" (A PBJ is a peanut butter and jelly sandwich—another Pike family favourite.)

"She just ate breakfast," I said, not budging from my bed.

"I know," my father said. "But she wants to have a picnic with her dolls in the back garden."

"Oh, all right."

I slammed my notebook shut and followed my father. I made Claire a sandwich as quickly as I could, then sliced it into little doll-sized triangles. This time I didn't even get to the kitchen door before my mother called me to do something else.

"Mal, darling, would you help me fold these clothes?"

"Mother!" I blew my hair off my forehead in exasperation. "I have to work on my story, you know."

"This will only take a minute. Then I promise to leave you alone."

It didn't take a minute. It took an hour because Margo got hit in the face with a shuttlecock from the badminton set. It didn't break her nose or anything, but it still hurt a lot. Mum had to comfort her and I had to make another lot of PBJs for Claire because the neighbours' dog came over and wolfed them all down when her back was turned.

Once I was back in my room, I tried to shut everything out of my mind except writing. But just when I'd have a possible story forming in my head, Dad or one of my brothers would interrupt and I'd have to start all over again. This went on *all* afternoon. I wanted to scream. I took my pen and scratched in big, bold letters on the top of my blue-lined notebook paper: *Two may be company, and three may be a crowd, but ten is a mob*!

"Mallory!" my mother called at six o'clock. "It's suppertime. Please come down and help me serve."

"Mallory!" I repeated, imitating my

mother in a singsong voice. "Wash the dishes, scrub the floors, take out the rubbish. Be my slave!"

I wanted to throw my notebook against the wall. Instead, I took a deep breath and tried to calm my temper.

I don't know why I felt so resentful about being asked to do chores. I've been doing them my whole life. I suppose I just felt as though I'd wasted a lot of things. Like my quarter. I'd paid Vanessa to leave me alone, and it was Mum and Dad who turned out to be the problem. And what about the rest of my day? Six hours of work on my story, and I had only written one sentence.

"At this rate," I muttered as I trudged down the steps, "I'll never finish it."

# 5th CHAPTER

Mr Dougherty's creative writing class meets on Tuesdays and Fridays in what used to be a staff room. I love walking into that room. Mr D. has filled it with plants and bookshelves crammed with books. It doesn't feel like a classroom at all. It's more like a comfortable library in someone's home. Every time I step through the door a little shiver of excitement runs through me, as if something wonderful is about to happen. Like maybe I'm really on my way to becoming a writer.

On Tuesday I wore my navy blue wool skirt and knitted tank top with a white starched blouse and penny loafers, so I would look more studious. It's extremely important to me that Mr Dougherty takes me seriously.

Mr D. was busy writing on the blackboard, and his back was turned to the room.

I took my usual place in the half circle arranged around his desk. Mr Dougherty says that makes our class more like a seminar, a type of class you get in college in which students exchange ideas with their teacher. Being in a seminar made all of us feel *very* mature and special.

Everyone in the class—there are ten of us—was at his or her desk long before the bell rang. We sat up straight in our seats, eager for the lesson to begin.

As the bell rang, Mr D. put down his chalk and turned to face us. He wore a brown corduroy jacket with suede patches at the elbows, a red-and-yellow-tartan shirt, and baggy beige trousers. (I personally think all teachers should dress that way. It makes them look very acute.)

" 'The Write Stuff,' " he declared, pointing at the words he'd written on the board. He smiled at us. "Have you got it?"

I folded my hands in front of me and swallowed hard. I certainly hoped so. The boy sitting beside me shuffled his feet and cleared his throat.

"Now, there's the right stuff in everyday life," Mr D. continued. "That's having the courage to do a physically dangerous job, like flying a space shuttle, or fighting forest fires." He paused dramatically. "And then there's the Write Stuff—which means having the creativity, the persistence, and the inner strength it takes to do the writing job." I held my breath as he walked in front of us, looking each one of us in the eye. Finally he said, "I think you've got it."

The room was filled with a sigh as the ten of us exhaled with relief.

"However," Mr Dougherty said, raising one finger, "it's something you have to work at. Being a writer takes a lot of self-discipline. You've got to *make* yourself work. No one can do it for you."

Boy, was that the truth! Other people always seemed to get in a writer's way. Like my family, who still wouldn't leave me alone long enough to let me write even a page.

Mr D. perched on the edge of his desk. "How many of you will be writing a piece for Young Authors Day?"

Ten of us raised our hands.

"Good." He twirled his moustache. "Let me take down your names so that I can arrange for enough teachers to read and judge your work."

We waited patiently as he scribbled down our names on a pad of yellow paper. When he had finished, Mr Dougherty looked back at the class.

"Today I want to talk to each of you individually about your entry," he said.

"While I'm doing that, I'd like the rest of you to pick an object in this room and make up a one-page history of that particular item. Where it came from, its name—if you care to name it—and how it ended up in this room."

Immediately everyone pulled pieces of paper out of their files, then sat nibbling on the ends of their pens while they stared around the room for a suitable object. I was trying to make up my mind between the slightly rusty wastepaper basket and the prickly cactus on the windowsill, when Mr D. called me to his desk.

"As I recall," he said, twirling his moustache and leaning back in his chair, "you said you were going to enter the Best Overall Fiction contest. Is that right, Mallory?"

"Yes, sir." I felt as if I was being tested, and my voice shook a little. It was silly for me to feel like that because Mr D. is so nice. But he's also an author, and at that moment he was talking to me, author to author, about my story.

"Tell me a little about the plot."

That was the one thing I had managed to work on between doing my chores, baby-sitting, and working on homework. "My story is about a girl named Tess. She comes from a large family and feels left out. Her mum and dad hardly seem to notice she's there. They're too worried about her older sister, who wants to go out with a boy they don't like, or her younger brothers, who are always getting into trouble at school. So, even though Tess is in the middle, she feels the farthest from their affection."

"Nicely phrased," Mr Dougherty said. "What happens to Tess?"

"Well, one day, her parents have to go away, and they leave her in charge. That's when Tess finds out how important she is to the family."

Mr D. stroked his moustache as he nodded his head. That made me feel good. But that only lasted a few seconds because then he asked to see what I had written.

I flipped open my notebook and stared down at the first page of my story. The blank spots looked huge and I tried to cover them with my hand, but it was too late.

"Three paragraphs?" he asked, raising an eyebrow. "That's all you've written?"

"Uh, I—I really haven't had a chance to write it yet," I stammered. "I've been pretty busy at home, and I've mostly been concentrating on the plot." It wasn't a lie. I really had been thinking about the plot.

Mr Dougherty took a deep breath and sighed. It was a disappointed sound, one that I would have given anything not to hear. "Thinking about your story is important for any author," he said quietly, "but until you actually put the words on the page, Mallory, you can't call yourself a writer."

I stared down at my notebook, too ashamed to look him in the eye. "I know that," I murmured. For one terrible moment, I thought I was going to cry. It took every ounce of willpower to stop myself. I just couldn't humiliate myself in front of Mr Dougherty and the whole class. It was too awful even to think about.

Mr Dougherty stood up, letting me know that our conference was over. He must have sensed how rotten I felt because he patted me on the shoulder and said, "I know you can write, Mallory. I just want to remind you that time is running out. Young Authors Day is only three weeks away."

I shut my notebook and clutched it to my chest. "Don't worry, Mr Dougherty," I said in a shaky voice I hardly recognized as my own. "I'm going to spend every spare minute working on this. I won't let you down."

My words echoed in my head walking home from school that day. I was afraid that I might actually let Mr Dougherty down, and then I'd never be able to face him again. As I climbed the steps to my front door, I decided to make a work schedule for myself and stick to it.

The minute I got into the house, I grabbed an apple from the fruit bowl on the kitchen worktop and headed straight up to my room. I dumped my books onto my bed and gathered some materials with which to make my schedule—two pieces of lined paper, some tape, a ruler, and coloured pens. Turning the two pieces of paper sideways, I taped them together and drew lines across them to make a graph. Then I listed each day leading to Young Authors Day down one side. Across the top I wrote the hours of the day after school. Here's what the first four days looked like:

| | 3:00 | 4:00 | 5:30 | 6:00 | 7:00 | 8:00 | 9:00 |
|---|---|---|---|---|---|---|---|
| Tues: | Baby-sit triplets | Homework | Dinner | my story | | | Bed |
| Wed: | Baby-sit Rodowskys | My Story | BSC | Dinner | Homework | | Bed |
| Thurs: | Homework | Chores | Dinner | My Story | | | Bed |
| Fri: | My Story | | BSC | Dinner | Homework | | Bed |

As I was busy working on the schedule, Vanessa came into the room and looked over my shoulder.

"What's that for?" she asked.

"For me. So I can be a disciplined, creative writer. "I used Mr D.'s exact words. "It's my schedule until Young Authors Day. What do you think?"

"It looks pretty heavy," Vanessa said. "When do you have time for fun?"

I looked back at my graph and realized I hadn't drawn in any time for talking on the phone to Jessi, or going to the shopping mall, or even stopping for a Coke. "I don't think I have time for fun," I decided. "This is too important."

Vanessa pointed to the first day on the schedule. "According to this, you're supposed to be doing your homework right now."

I looked at my watch. "You're right. Thanks, Vanessa. Tell the rest of the family not to bother me while I'm working, will you?"

"I think you can tell them yourself."

Vanessa pointed to Claire, who was standing in the doorway. She was holding her finger, which was wrapped in a dinosaur plaster. Behind her stood the triplets with devilish grins on their faces.

"They say all the dinosaurs died," Claire said in a tiny voice. "That's not true, is it?"

A talk with Claire always means trying to find answers to endless questions. It takes a lot of time and patience—two things I was short of at that moment. But her chin was quivering and her eyes were so full of tears that I couldn't tell her to go away.

"Come here and sit on my lap," I said, patting my knee, "and I'll tell you about the dinosaurs that lived in the past, and the ones that live in our minds now."

Claire smiled triumphantly at her brothers and then marched over to my side.

"Oh, Mal," my mother called from down the hall. A moment later her head appeared in the doorway. "I'm glad I caught you. Would you mind making the dessert for dinner tonight, darling? I've got a thousand calls to make for the library board meeting, and I'll never get to it in time." She brushed a strand of hair off her forehead and smiled at me gratefully. "I'd really appreciate it if you could."

Just then I felt the way Claire had looked when she came to my door. All quivery inside. It was clear that I wasn't going to get to my homework before dinner, and I would have to do it during the time slot I had reserved to work on my story. It just wasn't fair. I felt like screaming, "No! I can't! And I won't! Get someone else!"

But I didn't.

"Of course, Mum. What do you want me to make?"

"Chocolate chip cookies!" Claire squealed, wrapping her arms around my neck.

"All right," I murmured forlornly. "Chocolate chip cookies."

# 6th CHAPTER

Peace and quiet. At last!

It was Friday afternoon. I had spent most of the week trying to stick to my writing schedule and not being able to do it. After I'd said goodbye to Jessi, I went straight home and shut myself in my room.

Nobody—not Vanessa, not Mum and Dad, not even Claire—interrupted me while I worked on my story. Can you believe it? And, boy, did I work! I focused all my attention on writing, and everything around me seemed to disappear. All the sounds in the house and all my worries about school and family just melted away.

I was on a roll. Five pages straight! I hope this doesn't sound conceited, but they were good pages, too. My story was really starting to come together, and just as I was thinking that I could probably write another five pages, I glanced at the clock. It was 5:30 on the dot.

"Yikes!" I leaped out of my chair. "The BSC. I forgot all about it!"

As I told you, we meet every Monday, Wednesday, and Friday at *exactly* 5:30. And if anyone is late (as I was about to be), Kristy gets miffed.

As I was putting away my notebook, a funny feeling came over me. My story was very important to me, and if I could just keep working on it, I might be able to finish it in the next couple of days. I really resented having to drop everything to go to the BSC meeting. But I had made a commitment (as my mother always says) to the BSC. And if I didn't go, I would be letting my friends down. But what about my story?

I looked at the clock again. Five thirty-one. The meeting had already started. Right now Kristy and the others were probably wondering what had happened to me. In a minute, Jessi would probably phone to see if I was okay and then I'd have to stop writing anyway. I raced down the stairs, grabbed my bike, and pedalled as fast as I could to Claud's house.

"You're ten minutes late!" Kristy declared as I walked into the room. She didn't even ask why. Instead she made a big deal of looking at Claud's digital clock and shaking her head in disgust.

54

I had intended to apologize to the club, but Kristy made me angry. So I just kept my mouth shut and slumped down on the floor beside Jessi. She was leaning against Claud's bed with her knees pulled up under her chin.

Jessi gave me one of her "What's going on?" looks, but I still didn't say anything. I was angry with myself for being late, and angry with the BSC for taking me away from my writing. I needed time to sort things out.

Luckily for me, the phone rang and broke the silence in the room. Dawn got to it first.

"Babysitters Club. Oh, hello, Mrs Arnold." We listened as Dawn jotted down the details of the job and then said, "I'll phone you right back." She hung up the phone and announced, "Mrs Arnold needs a sitter for the twins tomorrow morning."

Kristy adjusted her visor and asked, "Who's available?"

Mary Anne tapped her pencil against her chin in thought. "Let's see. Dawn already has that job with the Rodowskys."

Kristy looked at me and said pointedly, "We assigned her the job at the start of the meeting." She didn't add, "Which you missed," but I know that's what she meant.

"And Jessi and Stacey are already

committed," Mary Anne continued. "How about Mal?" She smiled at me sympathetically. "You get along really well with the twins."

I didn't even have to hesitate. Saturday morning was out. I had scheduled the whole morning to work on my story.

"Sorry," I said. "I can't."

Jessi cocked her head in surprise. Usually I would have explained why, but I was still feeling crabby about the way Kristy had treated me.

"Okay," Mary Anne said, after a sideways glance at Kristy. "Then how about you, Claud?"

Claudia was trying to open a bag of M&M's with her teeth, without much success. "That'd be fine," she mumbled.

The phone rang two more times, and Mary Anne and Dawn accepted jobs for Saturday night with the Sobaks and the Addisons. I didn't feel so bad about that since, as a junior member, I can't really babysit at night anyway. Then Mrs Perkins phoned, and Jessi took a job on Sunday afternoon.

It wasn't a very fun meeting. Basically, we sat quietly between calls, watching Claud try to open the M&M's. At any other meeting, everybody would have cracked jokes about her being such a junk food addict, but not today. I knew it was my fault, but I couldn't seem to get out of my rotten mood.

Claud finally found a nail file in one of her drawers and gouged a hole in the side of the bag of sweets. "Voilà!" she cried. "Treats. Something to cheer us up."

She passed the bag around the room, and everyone except Dawn and Stacey took some. I suppose we needed cheering up.

The phone rang again and this time Stacey answered it. "It's the Perkinses. They need a sitter for Monday afternoon."

Mary Anne scanned the list again. "Well, Mal is the only one who hasn't taken a job today," she said. "I think she should have it."

I shook my head once more. "Sorry. I can't."

Kristy threw her hands up in exasperation. "What's going on, Mal? You've just turned down two perfectly good jobs. Don't you want to babysit?"

Everyone in the room was staring at me, and I knew it was now or never. I would have to tell them everything.

"Of course I do," I blurted out. "But I just can't take any jobs right now. I don't have time. I've got my homework and all my chores at home, plus the family is starting to drive me insane."

It was really weird. Once I finally let loose, the words just poured out.

"I never seem to get any privacy at home, and the deadline for Young Authors Day is less than two weeks away. I've just *got* to finish my story. My schedule doesn't even allow me to take a phone call, let alone a babysitting job."

"What schedule?" Kristy asked.

"The one I made up on Tuesday."

At first I had pinned the schedule to my notice board, but then I discovered I needed to carry it with me all the time so I would know what I was supposed to do next. It was in my back pocket.

"Here," I said, unfolding it and handing it to Kristy. "I've got something planned for every minute that I'm awake."

Kristy scanned it and then looked up at me. "Where's your time for baby-sitting?"

I pointed to the days and squares that I had marked. "It's all there. See? I scheduled the jobs I'm signed up for."

"What about new jobs?"

Uh-oh. "I suppose I didn't think about new jobs." I refolded the schedule and stuffed it back into the pocket of my jeans.

Once again Kristy exchanged serious looks with Mary Anne and the others. "You know, Mal, it's really important that we all be available to take jobs," she said. "If no one's free, then people will stop calling."

"I know that," I mumbled. "But my story . . ."

I didn't finish my sentence. I think my friends knew how important the story was to me. But the BSC was also important, and they wanted to make sure I didn't forget it.

There was another one of those awful silences where no one, especially me, knew where to look. Then finally the numbers on the clock clicked over and Claud, who had managed to devour nearly a whole bag of M&M's, said, "Six o'clock!"

Kristy nodded her head. "Then this meeting of the Babysitters Club is officially adjourned."

"Monday is subs day, everybody," Stacey reminded us, as we gathered up our bags. "Don't forget to bring your money next time."

Jessi and I walked down the hall. We didn't talk. I could tell she was waiting for me to tell her what was wrong, but I didn't know where to start.

I felt awful. I wasn't being a good club member. I had broken one of the first rules of the BSC by being late. Instead of apologizing, I'd been resentful that I'd had to go to the meeting. A little voice inside my head wondered if maybe I should take leave of absence. Just for a while, until Young Authors Day was over. But I was too afraid to bring it up. Kristy had not reacted well to my being late, and she'd been upset when I turned down the two jobs. I was afraid she might suggest I resign from the club altogether.

I decided to keep my mouth shut and not mention the thought to anyone. Not even to Jessi.

# 7th
# CHAPTER

"Watch me ride the pony!" five-year-old Suzi Barrett cried, as she galloped past me into the Barretts' living room.

Her brother, Buddy, who is eight, followed close on her heels, shouting, "I'm the sheriff. And I'm going to arrest you for speeding!" Buddy was wearing his cowboy hat, a T-shirt, and jeans.

Mrs Barrett had scheduled this sitting job two weeks earlier. Otherwise I would have been at home, working on my story. Instead, I was spending the afternoon with the Impossible Three.

Dawn had given the Barrett kids that nickname when she first starting sitting for them because they were so out of control. But the problem turned out to be Mrs Barrett, who had gone through a tough divorce. She was so busy trying to find a job and straighten out her own life that she didn't have much time or energy for her children.

Actually, the Barrett kids are really nice, but when the three of them get excited and want to play, disastrous things can happen.

I was sitting on the bottom step of the stairs in their past, trying to put shoes on two-year-old Marnie. She was wriggling all over and calling, "Play!" every time her brother and sister ran by us. I had just managed to tie Marnie's left shoe when I heard a loud crash from the kitchen.

"Uh-oh," I heard Suzi say.

"You're going to get it!" Buddy yelled.

I raced for the kitchen. Suzi met me in the doorway, her round tummy sticking out from under her T-shirt. Her eyes looked huge. "Buddy knocked over that bag of white stuff."

"Did not!" Buddy shouted. "It was Suzi!"

"Did too!" Suzi shot back. "You hit the bag when you ran by."

"What bag . . .?" My voice trailed off as I stepped into the kitchen. The floor was covered in a fine white powder. "Flour," I said with a groan. "It's everywhere."

Suzi grabbed my leg and cried, "I didn't do it."

I tried to hide my irritation by saying, "It

doesn't matter who did it, Suzi. Why don't we just clean it up?"

Marnie toddled into the room then and clapped her hands together in glee. "Snow!"

Before I could stop her, she ran onto the flour, slid, and fell flat on her back. The fall took her by surprise, so for a second she didn't cry. Then she opened her mouth and a loud wail filled the room.

"Buddy!" I cried. "Get a broom and a dustpan, will you? Suzi, help your brother, please, while I take care of Marnie."

I skated my way through the slippery flour, picked up Marnie, then inched over to the nearest chair and sat down.

"That was pretty scary, wasn't it?" I whispered. She nodded her head, then rubbed her hand across her eyes, leaving behind a white streak.

"I'm a good helper!" Suzi exclaimed, as she entered the kitchen with Buddy. "Watch me clear up."

She and her brother were struggling with a large red plastic bucket. I realized, too late, that it was full of water. I tried to stand up, but Marnie, who was still on my lap, had grabbed the phone cord and I fell back on the chair.

"Don't put that water on the floor!" I cried feebly.

"Don't worry," Buddy reassured me.

"We know what we're doing." Then he emptied the whole contents of the bucket onto the linoleum. "This is how Mum scrubs the floor."

I gasped in dismay as the water spread like a miniature tidal wave across the spilled flour. Buddy began pushing the mop back and forth furiously, and within seconds the mop head was choked with clumps of thick, white paste.

A loud bark came from the back door and Suzi yelled, "Pow wants to come in!" She opened the door and the Barretts' droopy old basset hound charged into the kitchen. He promptly skidded into the mess and covered himself in goo. Then he lumbered to his feet and shook his floppy ears from side to side, spraying bits of flour paste everywhere.

I managed to untangle myself from the phone cord. Then I put Marnie firmly on the chair, stood up, and cried, "Buddy! Suzi! Stop that immediately!"

I didn't mean to speak so loudly, but I had to stop them that instant. And I did. Buddy let go of the mop and it clattered to the floor. Suzi, who had been dancing around, trying to avoid getting her feet in the water, was so startled, she sat down in a big glob of sticky flour. Marnie stopped crying in midsob.

Buddy looked at me in confusion. "What'd I do wrong?"

I took a deep breath. "Buddy, you didn't do anything wrong. Neither did you, Suzi. You were both being very good helpers, but you can't clean up flour with water and a mop."

Suzi just stared at me with a worried frown on her forehead.

"What I mean is," I explained, "maybe this is a job for me to do. You two have helped enough."

"We have?" Suzi's round face spread into a big smile. "Good."

"Can I go outside and ride my bicycle?" Buddy asked.

"Okay," I said, helping Suzi to her feet. "But be careful of cars, stay close by, and take Pow with you."

"All right!" Buddy was out of the back door in a flash. I was relieved to have to deal with only two children and the gigantic mess.

Suzi agreed to take her clothes off in the laundry room, then go upstairs and change. Luckily Marnie hadn't got too much flour on her, so I was able to brush her off. I sat her in her high chair, put some Cheerios and some raisins on the tray, and then started working on the kitchen floor.

Twenty minutes later, the paste had gone but the floor still had a sort of filmy look to it. I ran a wet mop over it and hoped for the best. Then Suzi suggested we take Marnie to the family room to play with her dolls.

"Good idea," I said, lifting Marnie out of the high chair and following Suzi to the stairs. But before we could take two steps, a high-pitched cry pierced the air.

"Mallory! Help me!"

It was Buddy. I had almost forgotten about him. I handed Marnie to Suzi and said, "Wait right here." Then I raced outside.

Buddy's bike was lying on the pavement in front of the house. He was hobbling barefoot across the lawn towards the front door.

"Buddy," I cried, rushing to his side. "What on earth happened to you?"

He was so upset, he could barely talk. "I was c-c-coming down the hill," he said, hiccupping. "Really fast. And my foot got caught in the spokes."

Buddy held his right foot out to me and I nearly fainted. It was covered with blood. I couldn't tell how badly it had been cut but, without going into gory details, it looked absolutely terrible.

I scooped Buddy up in my arms and hurried back into the kitchen. My heart was pounding in my chest, and I kept saying over and over to myself, "Don't panic. Don't panic."

Suzi and Marnie were standing side by side in the kitchen, their faces as pale as their brother's.

"I'm going to sit you down in this chair, Buddy," I said, pulling one out from the table with my foot, "and then I'm going to wrap your foot in a clean towel. All right?"

Buddy, who had stopped sobbing, just nodded as I settled him in the chair. I remembered from my first aid class that I was supposed to elevate his foot, so I grabbed another chair and slid it under his heel. Then I ran into the hall and found a clean white towel in the linen cupboard.

Suzi and Marnie hadn't moved a muscle. Finally Suzi asked, "What happened?"

"Your brother's had an accident," I told her. I lifted Buddy's foot gently and wrapped it in the towel, remembering to apply as much pressure as possible to stop the bleeding. "I need you to be brave and take care of Marnie for me while I phone the doctor. Can you do that?"

Suzi swallowed hard and nodded.

"Good. Why don't you take Marnie into the living room and look in my Kid-Kit?" I suggested. "I've got some new colouring books you can show her."

"All right." Suzi's voice was barely audible. She took Marnie by the hand and led her out of the room.

My head was spinning. I went to the fridge and poured Buddy a glass of apple juice and pressed it into his hand. "Here,

Buddy, drink this. It'll make you feel better. I'm going to make a few calls."

He took a long drink, then said, "Thank you."

I picked up the phone and listened to the dialling tone buzzing in my ear. I couldn't decide whether to call 999 or my mother. Then I heard a commotion at the front door.

"Mummy! Mummy!" Suzi cried, rushing into the hall. "Buddy's hurt. There's blood everywhere!"

"What?" Mrs Barrett rushed into the kitchen, dropping several bags of groceries onto the floor. Buddy took one look at his mother and started crying all over again.

"Oh, Buddy!" she said, hugging him tightly. "You're going to be all right." Then she looked at me and said in a tight voice, "Mallory. What's happened here?"

I drew in a deep breath and tried to keep my voice from shaking too much as I explained. "Buddy was outside riding his bike and caught his foot in the spokes."

Mrs Barrett knelt next to the chair and carefully unwrapped the towel. "Where are his shoes?"

"I wasn't wearing any," Buddy replied with a sob.

"What?" his mother and I said at the same time.

When I saw him on the lawn I had

assumed he'd kicked off his shoes after the accident. I'd had no idea that he was barefoot when I let him go outside. I was so busy with Marnie and the flour mess that I hadn't checked him properly. I felt terrible.

"Should I call the doctor?" I asked, trying to hold back my tears.

Mrs Barrett examined Buddy's foot carefully. "The cut's on his heel. It's not very deep." She looked up at me and smiled thinly. "Luckily, it looks worse than it is. I don't think he needs to see a doctor."

"But it hurts, Mum," Buddy protested.

"I know it does, darling," Mrs Barrett said, giving him another warm hug. "And I'm going to go to the medicine cabinet and find something to make it feel better." She stood up and added, "Mallory, could you watch Suzi and Marnie for a few more minutes until I take care of this?"

"Of course," I answered. "I'll stay as long as you need me."

Just then, I felt so awful that I was willing to move in with them. Anything to make up for being such an irresponsible babysitter.

Fifteen minutes later, everything had returned to normal. Buddy was hopping around as if nothing had happened, a shiny plaster on his heel.

After Mrs Barrett had paid me, I apologized again for letting Buddy get hurt.

"Don't be too hard on yourself, Mallory," she said, as I left the house. "These things happen."

Maybe they do, I thought to myself, but not to *good* babysitters.

A good babysitter would not have let Buddy go outside without his shoes. That accident would never have happened if I had been paying attention.

## 8th CHAPTER

Tuesday

It's always fun sitting for the Pike family. Partly because Mal is my best friend. But mostly because I like the kids. Margo and Claire are always doing something creative and unusual. This Tuesday was no exception. They had got into the clothes trunk, but instead of just playing ordinary dressing up, they decided to stage their own ballet. I helped them work on the story, and even taught them a few steps. But they got carried away with their story and what started out as fun turned out to be sort of cruel. I really wanted to talk to Mallory about it, since the story centered around her, but I didn't have the nerve. So Mal, when you read this, please realize that I'm sorry about what happened and I shouldn't have let it get so out of hand.

Jessi came to babysit for Claire and Margo, her Kid-Kit under her arm. I had an appointment with the orthodontist, and while he tightened my brace (Ow!) Mum took the rest of the kids shopping for clothes and shoes.

Claire met Jessi with a gleeful hug at the door.

"Boy, are we glad to see you!" Margo said.

Jessi was a little surprised at their greeting since they saw her almost every day. "Well, I'm really glad to see you two, too!" she replied with a smile. She set her Kid-Kit on the floor. "I brought something special for you today."

"Me first!" Claire cried, reaching for the kit. "Let me see first." She opened the box and held up a doll. "Ooooh, Sindy!"

"Why don't we take Sindy out on the front steps?" Jessi suggested. "It's such a nice day. Then I'll show you what else I've brought."

Jessi had put some picture books of horses in the box, along with several of her favourite animal puppets. At the last minute she had added the flowered crown that she had worn in the ballet *Coppélia*.

Jessi had also included a brand-new box of coloured chalk, which Margo found immediately. "Let's play hopscotch!" she said, running for the drive.

"Me first!" Claire shouted as she followed her sister down the concrete drive.

Margo drew several boxes in blue chalk and then decided to try the pink and green. Claire looked on approvingly. "A rainbow," she said.

Margo turned to Jessi and asked, "Would you play, too, Jessi?"

"Of course," Jessi replied. "I love hopscotch."

They each chose a flat stone from the side of the drive.

"We like playing with *you*," Margo declared.

Claire nodded in agreement. "Much better than mean old Mallory."

Jessi looked surprised. "Why do you call her that?"

Claire tossed her stone and hopped two squares. "She's not nice."

"She never lets us in her room any more," Margo added, "and she's always ordering us around."

Claire crossed her arms and stuck out her lower lip. "She's a big grouch."

"Well, I'm sure she doesn't mean to upset you," Jessi said, tossing her own stone and hopping three squares. "Maybe her teeth are hurting her."

I know Jessi was just trying to be nice and make excuses for me. Let's face it, I *had* been a big grump with everyone, even with Jessi, my best friend.

"Your sister's always having her brace adjusted, and that can be pretty painful," Jessi continued, but Margo and Claire didn't look convinced.

"If her teeth hurt," Margo said, tossing

her stone onto a square, "she should tell us."

"I don't want her to tell me," Claire announced as she took her turn. "I don't want to talk to her."

"You stepped on the line," Margo pointed out to her sister.

"Did not!" Claire shot back.

Margo turned to Jessi. "What do you think?"

"I didn't see it," Jessi said diplomatically, "but I'll tell you what. Why don't you take another turn, Claire, and Margo and I will both watch closely."

This time Claire managed not to step on the line, and she smiled triumphantly at her sister. "See?"

Even though she tried hard not to win, Jessi did anyway. When Margo suggested they play again, Claire shook her head.

"No. I want a new game," she declared.

Claire went back to the Kid-Kit and found the puppets, then held up the crown of flowers. "What's this?"

"That's the crown I wore in *Coppélia*," Jessi explained. She performed an *arabesque*, her leg suspended in the air behind her, and then stepped into a curtsy.

"Ballet!" Claire cried, putting the crown on her head. "Let's make a ballet!"

Margo, who loves playing dressing up,

took up the cry. "A ballet! And we can wear costumes and everything."

My family keeps a trunk full of old clothes in the TV room, just for that purpose. Before Jessi knew what was happening, Margo and Claire had taken her by the hands and pulled her inside the house.

"The puppets can be in the show, too!" On one hand, Margo put the Fozzie Bear puppet that was missing one eye, and on the other, she put the Kermit the frog puppet.

Claire had opened the trunk. She held up some faded chiffon dresses that had belonged to our grandmother. "Ballet dresses."

Jessi grinned. "They're beautiful. But you should know that in a ballet the dresses are called *tutus*."

"I thought those were short and made of that scratchy stuff," Margo said.

"Netting?" Jessi laughed. "Yes, they are, but a *tutu* can be long or short."

"Toot toot!" Claire danced around the room in a long pink satin gown. Or I should say, tried to dance. The dress was much too big, and she tripped on the material with every step.

Margo pulled a blue chiffon dress over her head. It looked like a party dress from the nineteen-fifties. (Jessi thought for half a second that Claud might really like it, too. Claudia is very into fifties styles.)

"Now what should our ballet be about?" Jessi asked, as she rummaged through a stack of records lying beside an old record player.

"A beautiful girl!" Margo cried, spinning in a circle.

"*Two* beautiful girls," Claire said, imitating her sister. She threw her arms out to the sides and did three turns, which made her so dizzy she fell on the carpet, giggling.

Then Margo held up the bear puppet with the missing eye and said, "Two beautiful girls, and their mean old sister—"

"Mallory!" Claire giggled, sitting up.

Jessi, who had found an album of *The Nutcracker Suite* and was putting the record on the turntable, spun round. She felt she ought to discourage them from saying horrible things about their own sister. On the other hand, she thought maybe they would feel better if they acted out their frustration with Mallory.

"What should we call this, um, ballet?" Jessi asked as she placed the needle on the first song on the second side. She knew that the "Waltz of the Flowers" was perfect music for dancing.

Margo moved the bear puppet's mouth as

she spoke in a high voice. "Let's call it *Mean Old Mallory*."

"That's good!" Claire stood on top of the trunk. "And this will be the castle."

Margo climbed up beside her sister. "And we're the beautiful princesses trapped in the castle by—" She held up the puppet. "Mean Old Mallory."

"Mean Old Mallory!" Claire stuck out her tongue at the bear puppet, which Margo made bite her on the nose. Claire grabbed her nose and said, "Ow, that hurt."

Jessi couldn't help giggling. The two girls looked as if they had been rehearsing their comedy routine for weeks. Then Jessi remembered that they were making fun of her best friend, so she tried very hard not to let them see her laughing.

"All right, princesses!" Margo spoke in her high puppet voice. "I want you to dance around the castle and then clear your room."

"No!" Claire stamped her foot in defiance.

Margo made the bear puppet wag its hand at Claire. "And I want you to be quiet. You're really getting on my nerves."

Jessi forced herself to keep a straight face, which was hard because Margo sounded just like me when I'm grumpy.

"But why do we have to be quiet, Mean

Old Mallory?" Claire demanded. She was talking very realistically to the puppet.

"Because I have to get my teeth tightened."

"Teeth tightened?" This time Jessi couldn't stop herself from doubling up with laughter on the sofa.

Claire turned round with a big grin on her face. "Jessi thinks we're funny!"

"I think you're very funny," Jessi said, sitting up. "All of you."

"You'd better stop laughing," Margo said in her Mean Old Mallory voice, as she made the puppet shake its fist at Jessi. "Or I'll ask you to scrub the floors and then you won't be able to go to the ball."

Margo had turned the ballet of *Mean Old Mallory* into a strange form of *Cinderella*. Jessi sat back on the sofa, quietly watching to see which way the story would go next.

The ballet soon became a mixture of *Cinderella*, the game Mother May I?, and *The Three Little Pigs*. Claire would ask, "Mean Old Mallory, may I dance on the rug?" and Margo would say, "No! And if you do, I'll huff, and I'll puff, and I'll blow your crown off!"

The record came to an end and Claire, who was starting to get tired of being told no all the time, suddenly called, "They're home!"

Jessi listened carefully and could just make out the sound of a car engine. "Boy, that's good hearing, Claire!"

"Come on," Claire said, picking up big bunches of the pink satin material in front of her so she could run. "Let's go and tell Moozie!"

"Tell Moozie what?" Jessi asked.

"About our ballet," Margo finished. "*Mean Old Mallory.*"

"Oh, no!" Jessi reached the top of the stairs just in time to see the triplets bolt into the living room, clutching their new trainers. "You got my pair," Jordan was shouting at Byron.

Nicky was right behind the triplets, wearing a brand-new pair of loafers. Vanessa and I staggered in next, clutching bags full of T-shirts, new jeans, and socks.

Jessi tried to keep Claire from talking, but she couldn't reach her.

"Mal, guess what?" Claire squealed. "Jessi and Margo and I made up a ballet about you."

Jessi groaned and tried to look inconspicuous.

"It was about two beautiful princesses," Claire continued, "and their awful sister who's always yelling at them."

"Their sister was a real grouch because she had to write this story and have her brace fixed," Margo added. "So she wouldn't let them go to the ball or anything."

My mother came in from the hall just in time to hear Claire and Margo's story. "Now, girls, that's not funny."

"Jessi thought it was funny," Claire said. "She laughed so hard she fell over."

"It was their dancing that was funny," Jessi tried to say. But Claire kept right on talking.

"Guess what we called the ballet?" she added, giggling. "*Mean Old Mallory!*"

That was it. I'd had it with the triplets arguing in the shop over who got which shoes. I'd had it with Nicky shouting out license plate numbers in the car. I'd had it with my family, with my friends, with everyone. On top of it all, my teeth really did hurt. I turned to Claire and yelled, "Oh, shut up!"

Jessi watched along with the rest of the family as I bolted out of the kitchen and ran up the stairs to my room. She winced when she heard me slam the door. Mum looked questioningly at Jessi, but Jessi could only shrug. She didn't know what to say. Or do.

As my best friend, she knew she ought to march up to my room and try to explain everything. But she hesitated. *Mal's so upset,* she thought. *What if I try to talk to her and we get into an argument? That would only make things worse.*

After a few awkward moments, Jessi said, "Well, I suppose I'll get my Kid-Kit and go home. Would you ask Mal to phone me later, Mrs Pike?"

"Of course," said Mum.

Jessi walked down the steps of our house, feeling confused and hurt. The game she had hoped would be helpful had backfired, and now her best friend was angry with her and she didn't know what to do about it.

# 9th
# CHAPTER

"The Wednesday meeting of the Baby-sitters Club is officially called to order," Kristy said as the numbers on Claud's clock changed from 5:29 to 5:30.

I had arrived ten minutes early, but that didn't make my stomach feel any better. It was doing flip-flops inside me. I had made a very important decision, and the time had come to break the news to my friends.

Kristy was dressed in track suit bottoms and a T-shirt that said, "Go Krushers!" on the front. She flipped up her visor and asked, "Is there any new club business to discuss?"

I wanted to make my announcement, but I hesitated.

"The club notebook isn't quite up to date," Kristy continued. "No one has written in it for a few days."

Claud winced. "I'm one of the guilty ones. I had two jobs this week and I haven't written a word."

Kristy, in her stern chairman's voice, said, "We *have* to keep the notebook up to date. Because," she flashed a big smile, "that's one of the things that helps make us such great babysitters."

I wished she hadn't said that. My stomach did a triple somersault.

Stacey was holding the manila envelope containing the subs in her lap. "We're in good shape moneywise," she said, "so if anyone wants to buy new supplies for their Kid-Kits, let me know next Friday."

"I can't believe I heard Stacey McGill say that," Dawn joked to the rest of the club. "Old Scrooge?"

Everyone burst out laughing at the look on Stacey's face. Everyone except me, that is. Their laughter just made me feel worse.

"I am not a scrooge," Stacey protested, putting her hands on her hips. She tilted her head up and said, with as much dignity as she could master, "I'm just frugal."

Of course that made everyone laugh even more. I looked at the clock. Five minutes had passed. The calls from clients wanting to book jobs would start coming in any second, so it was now or never. I had to make my announcement. I raised my hand.

"Excuse me, everyone, but I've got an important announcement to make." My heart was pounding in my chest.

"Is it about Miss Frugal?" Claudia giggled, nudging Stacey in the ribs. Stacey swatted at her to stop, but she was grinning.

I closed my eyes and said the words really fast. "It's about me and the BSC. I would like to be demoted."

There was dead silence. Finally Kristy spoke.

"You're kidding, aren't you?"

I opened my eyes and shook my head. "No."

Jessi, who was sitting next to me, grabbed my hand. "Mallory, that's silly."

I looked Jessi square in the face. "I've done a lot of thinking about this, and I just don't feel I'm qualified to be a member. I really think you should make me an associate member, like Shannon or Logan."

Everyone started talking at once, trying to convince me to change my mind. Finally Kristy put her fingers to her lips and whistled loudly for everyone to be quiet. Then she turned to me and asked, "Why do you think you're not qualified to be in the BSC?"

"I'm a terrible sitter. Last week I wasn't paying close attention, and Buddy Barrett nearly cut his foot off."

"That could have happened to any of us," Mary Anne said.

"But it didn't. It happened to me. All because I wasn't paying attention."

"Maybe," Kristy cut in. "But when you saw that he was hurt, what did you do?"

"I carried him into the kitchen, made sure his foot was raised, then wrapped it, applying pressure to make the bleeding stop," I said, rattling off my answer like a paragraph out of a first aid book.

Kristy nodded solemnly. "You did everything right. I'd say you're a very good sitter."

"But I'm a terrible club member. Look at last week. I was late and didn't even apologize."

"Okay." Dawn leaned forward on the bed. "But you told us about the story you're writing and the pressure you're under at home, and we understood."

The rest of the girls in the room murmured their agreement with Dawn.

"But I'm not able to take any new jobs. And you've already had to call an associate member to take my place. Let's face it, I'm really letting you down."

"Mal, that's just not true!" Jessi protested.

"Besides, every job you turn down just means more money for us," Claud teased.

"That's right!" Kristy agreed, but I didn't feel any better. In fact, I felt worse. I was making my friends work harder and they were trying to make me feel good about it.

"You're just overloaded," Mary Anne said, smiling sympathetically. "You'll be able to take more jobs soon. I just know it."

"I don't know when I'll be able to take another job," I said, my voice getting tighter and louder. "So please demote me. If you don't, I'll resign!"

There. I'd said it. Jessi gasped in horror. Mary Anne's eyes instantly filled with tears. Claud dropped the bar of chocolate she was unwrapping onto her lap and stared at me, openmouthed.

"Resign?" Stacey and Dawn repeated in barely a whisper.

Kristy sat very still. No one had ever voluntarily resigned from the BSC. It was unthinkable.

The silence that followed my announcement was agony. Luckily, the phone rang. Claud answered it in a very subdued voice. She nodded her head several times, murmuring, "Mm hmm," then hung up. "The Prezziosos need a sitter for Thursday."

Mary Anne sniffed loudly as she examined the work schedule. "It looks as if Dawn can take that one."

Dawn nodded, and Claudia called Mrs Prezzioso back. The phone rang several more times, and everyone carried on mechanically, answering the phone and speaking in a monotone. I hadn't realized how my announcement would affect the club. I hadn't realized how hard it would hit me. I felt hollow inside.

Five minutes before the meeting was over, Kristy adjusted her visor and sat up in her chair. "Mal, I think you need time to think about this. So I propose that you take two weeks off from the club and babysitting."

"But what about—"

Kristy answered my question before I could ask it. "The rest of us will cover for you. That way you can finish your story and have some time to think things over."

Jessi, who looked sadder than I had ever seen her, turned to me and whispered, "Please say yes, Mal."

I glanced at Jessi and then back at Kristy. I still didn't feel good about letting the others carry my workload, but I really didn't want to leave the club. "All right," I murmured, "I'll try it."

"Good!" Kristy said as the numbers of the digital clock turned from 5:59 to 6:00. "Then we'll see you back here in two weeks.

And this meeting of the Babysitters Club is adjourned."

Two weeks seemed like an eternity. I felt as if I were about to take a long trip all by myself, and it made me feel sad. And lonely.

# 10th CHAPTER

Saturday

Boy, Mel, I think I got a small taste of what you've been going through at your house. On Saturday morning my mom found out that a friend of hers had a heart attack. She and Watson rushed to the hospital and left me with David Michael, Emily Michelle, Karen, and Andrew. Emily Michelle was cranky because she hadn't eaten lunch yet. Karen and Andrew wanted to go outside and play, but it was pouring with rain. Then David Michael's new friend, Carver, came to the door with his parents and it was all downhill from there....

Watson Brewer's home is a mansion. Even with Kristy and her three brothers, her new sister, and her grandmother, it never feels crowded. That's why it's nice when Kristy's little stepsister and stepbrother come to stay. They make the mansion seem more full.

Usually Kristy loves spending time with Karen and Andrew. But she had already made plans to spend Saturday with Mary Anne. She'd reserved the evening for her stepbrother and stepsister.

Kristy had just put on her yellow anorak and was about to leave to meet Mary Anne when Watson burst into the entrance hall, explaining about the phone call he had just received.

"Sorry," he added, as he pulled his trench coat off its hook and grabbed an umbrella from the stand, "but your mother and I have to go over to Stoneybrook General. Fourth floor. Intensive care. Watch the children."

"Wait a minute," Kristy protested. "Why can't Nannie do it?"

"She's bowling," her mother reminded her. As Mrs Brewer snatched her own coat and scarf, she added, "And Sam and Charlie are with their friends."

Kristy bit her lower lip in frustration. She was already running late to meet Mary Anne. "But when will you be back?"

"We don't know."

The front door shut and Watson and her mother had gone.

Kristy felt as if the rug had been pulled out from under her. Watson hadn't even said, "Please." He'd just given her an order, and suddenly she had to cancel her plans.

Emily Michelle was standing in the hall, clutching her teddy bear. Her parents had left without even saying goodbye to her. A tear ran down her cheek as she looked up at Kristy and said, "Cookie."

"All right, Emily." Kristy scooped her sister up in her arms and carried her into the kitchen. "Let's go and phone Mary Anne. Then we'll both have a cookie. Maybe that will make us feel better."

Moments later, Emily was sitting on the kitchen worktop, happily munching on a chocolate chip cookie, when Karen ran in, followed closely by David Michael, who was carrying a jar full of his latest collection of beetles.

"Tell David Michael to leave me alone!" Karen cried.

David Michael, grinning devilishly, said, "What's wrong, Karen? Don't you like having a jar full of beetles in your face?"

Andrew flew into the room with a towel pinned to his shoulders. "I'm Superboy," he cried. "I'll save you."

"Oh, no, you don't!" David Michael held up his jar full of beetles, like a shield. "These beetles are magic and can suck all your power out of you."

Emily Michelle studied the beetles and her face clouded up again. "*Waaaaaah!*"

"Everybody, be quiet!" Kristy shouted over the hubbub. "You're scaring Emily Michelle."

Normally that would have shut the kids up—if the doorbell hadn't rung.

"That's for me!" David Michael shouted. "My friend Carver Ensign is coming over to play."

"What?" Kristy cried. "Nobody told me about this." She was already entertaining four children. Five was pushing the limit.

"Mum said it was okay," David Michael called over his shoulder as he galloped towards the front door. Andrew and Karen hurried after him, anxious to see the visitor. Emily Michelle forgot about her tears and demanded, "Down!"

Kristy put her on the floor, and she followed her brothers and sister into the big entrance hall. David Michael opened the door and Boo-Boo, Watson's fourteen-pound cat, tore into the house, nearly tripping Emily up in the process. He was soaked from being caught in the rain.

Carver, a blond-haired boy with glasses,

stood in front of his parents in the front porch. "Hi, David Michael," he said, rubbing his hand across his nose.

"Come on in." David Michael swung back the big front door to reveal his four brothers and sisters, Boo-Boo the cat, and their dog, Shannon, who had trotted in from the living room to see what all the commotion was about. They stood in a tight clump, as if they were posing for a family portrait.

Carver's mother took one look at all the kids and pets and asked, "Where are your parents, David Michael?"

"They had to go to the hospital," Kristy said, grabbing Emily by the back of her pink dungarees to keep her from running out of the door. "I'm David Michael's sister, Kristy."

Instead of saying, "How do you do?" or "Pleased to meet you," Mrs Ensign turned to her husband and frowned. "Oh, dear, I thought his parents would be here."

"It was an emergency," Kristy explained, feeling a little irritated that the Ensigns were ignoring her. "Otherwise, I'm sure my mother would have phoned you."

"Come on, Carver," David Michael said. "I'll show you our house. It's huge. It's even got a second floor."

"That might be haunted," Karen added mysteriously. She has a pretty wild imagination and likes to believe that the attic is haunted by the ghost of Old Ben Brewer, her great-grandfather.

"A ghost!" Carver cried with glee. "Let's go and look."

"Hold on a minute, son." Mr Ensign put his hand on the boy's shoulder. "You know how your mother and I feel about your playing without adult supervision."

Kristy could feel the tips of her ears turning pink. What did they think she was? An irresponsible kid? She wanted to inform them that not only had she been babysitting practically forever, but she was also the chairman of the Baby-sitters Club. However, she decided to keep silent.

"Awww, Dad!" Carver dug the tip of his tennis shoe into the welcome mat. "Then, can David Michael come to our house?"

Mrs Ensign knelt down beside her son and smiled. "That's a good idea."

"An *excellent* idea!" David Michael cheered.

This time it was Kristy's turn to hesitate. She didn't think her parents would like the idea of her letting David Michael go off with strangers.

"I'm sorry, Mr and Mrs Ensign," Kristy said in what she hoped was a very mature voice. "But my parents left me in charge of my brothers and sisters. I'd have to get their permission before I could let David Michael go with you."

"What?" David Michael turned to face her indignantly. "You know they'd say yes. Come on, Kristy, please?"

Kristy shook her head. "I'm sorry, but I have to say no."

Carver's parents murmured that they understood. As they hurried through the rain back to their car, Mr Ensign said to his son, "Maybe another day, Carver. When David Michael's parents are at home."

"David Michael," Kristy began, "I'm sorry but—"

Her brother cut her off by slamming the front door as hard as he could. "I'm never speaking to you again for as long as I live!" he shouted. Then he ran up the stairs two at a time. Moments later, the house echoed with the slam of his bedroom door.

Kristy felt terrible. First her own parents had ordered her to babysit without any notice. Then the Ensigns had made her feel as if she were some little kid who couldn't handle responsibility. Now her brother was being rotten to her.

The other kids picked up on David Michael's foul mood at once.

"Let's go outside and play-ay," Andrew whined. "It's no fun in here."

Kristy stared miserably out of the window at the rain. "It's pouring outside, Andrew. Where would you play?"

"In the mud puddles," Karen cried. "Please, can't we go outside?"

"Out!" Emily chimed in.

Normally Kristy might have found umbrellas and anoraks for everyone, but Emily Michelle had had an earache the week before. Kristy didn't want to risk another one.

"I've got an idea!" Kristy tried to look enthusiastic. "Why don't we go to the attic and see if Old Ben Brewer's been there lately?"

That seemed to do the trick. Everyone trooped up the stairs to the attic with Karen in the lead. "We need to wear Ghost Detective outfits," she announced. (Karen just loves to dress up.)

Kristy thought that sounded like a great idea until Karen and Andrew started arguing over who got to wear the Sherlock Holmes cap that belonged to Watson, and who would carry Nannie's magnifying glass.

"You'll take turns!" Kristy said, switching Emily from one hip to the other. To top things off, Emily insisted on being carried everywhere, which only made Kristy more irritable than before.

The ghost hunt lasted for nearly an hour,

with Andrew and Karen fussing over everything. Then it was lunchtime, and no one could agree on what to eat.

"Look, you're all getting ham and cheese sandwiches," Kristy declared. "And that's final."

Unfortunately, the phone rang while Kristy was in the middle of making the sandwiches. She ran to answer it, leaving the ham unattended on the worktop.

"It's me," Mary Anne said. "Have they come back yet?"

Kristy could tell by the background noises that Mary Anne was in a shop. "No, but I wish they would hurry. We're all in bad moods."

"Well, if they come back any time soon," Mary Anne continued, "I'll be at Bellair's—"

Mary Anne's final words were cut off by a scream from Kristy. Boo-Boo was perched on the worktop, carefully removing the sliced ham from each sandwich and devouring it.

"Get away from there!" Kristy shouted, dropping the phone.

Boo-Boo's big yellow eyes widened, and he leaped for the kitchen table as Kristy approached him. Meanwhile, Andrew had just finished pouring himself a glass of milk from the fridge. Kristy's shout startled him and he dropped the glass, which shattered as it hit the floor.

"Andrew, *don't move!*" Kristy shouted.

"Kristy? What's the matter?"

Mary Anne's voice sounded tinny in the receiver, which was dangling by its cord close to the floor. Kristy grabbed the phone and said, "Mary Anne, I'm sorry but I've got to go. We're having a disaster here. I'll see you later." She hung up and carried Andrew out of the kitchen.

"Don't worry, I'll clear this up." Kristy tried to keep her voice calm. "Now, go back into the study and *sit down*."

"But we're hungry," Andrew complained. "We want our ham 'n' cheese sandwiches."

"Boo-Boo ate your sandwiches," Kristy said. "So we're changing the menu." She set him down by the doorway and declared, "Now we're having PBJs."

"Oh, boy!" Andrew said, running into the study. "They're my favourite."

"Good." Kristy tried to smile but she couldn't. She felt too frazzled. Finally she knelt down and carefully picked the pieces of glass out of the spilled milk.

"Now I know what Mallory's life must be like every day," Kristy grumbled out loud to Boo-Boo, who was hiding under the table. "I don't envy her one bit."

She swept the broken glass into a dustpan and carried it to the rubbish bin. Then she wiped up the milk with a sponge. Kristy tried to imagine always having to be responsible for so many brothers and sisters, then trying to find time to work. She murmured, "No wonder Mal is thinking about giving up the BSC."

Kristy squeezed the sponge out in the sink and paused. It was hard to picture the Babysitters Club without one of its members. "I certainly hope she doesn't resign. Where would I find another baby-sitter as good as Mallory?"

# 11th CHAPTER

I groped for my glasses on the bedside table and read the numbers on the bedside clock. It was 8:00 on Saturday morning.

"Perfect," I murmured drowsily. "I've got the whole day to write."

I'd finished my homework the night before, and I was really looking forward to writing "Caught in the Middle." (That's the title I had chosen.) I lay back against my pillow and thought about the cover that I would design for my story. Mr Dougherty had told us that the pupils who submitted a story would also have to make a cover for it. Some kids were going to make theirs out of construction paper, but I had a different idea.

I thought about making a collage of kids doing all sorts of activities, with my main character, Tess, in the middle. I thought I could probably find some good pictures in magazines, but I also knew that we had some terrific photos in our family album. I thought about the picture of the triplets beaming at the camera from their high chairs, with creamed spinach smeared all over their faces and hair. My dad took a great photo of Margo when she was two, in just a nappy, standing in my mother's high heels and holding a handbag. One of my favourites was of Nicky as a baby, sound asleep in the laundry basket.

I lay in bed, smiling to myself and thinking about the photos—deciding that maybe I wouldn't cut out photos from magazines, maybe I would just use photos of my family—when I was suddenly seized by fear. Fear that this weekend with my family would be like all the others.

"Tying shoelaces, making snacks, running errands, settling arguments, searching for plasters!" I said loud. "I can't do that!"

"What are you saying?" Vanessa asked from the next bed.

"I'm saying *no*!" I threw back my covers and sat up. "No to everyone. Today is *my* day. It has to be. I'm running out of time."

"Time?" Vanessa mumbled drowsily.

"Young Authors Day is a week away and—" Suddenly it was as if a light bulb had been turned on inside my head. "I've got an idea." I moved into high gear, tossing off my nightdress and pulling on a pair of jeans and a sweat shirt. Then I dived under the bed.

"What are you doing?" Vanessa sat up, wide awake now.

"I'm . . . oh, ugh!" I choked as I nearly inhaled a big dust ball. I made a mental note to clear up my room as soon as Young Authors Day was over. "I'm looking for that yellow poster board I stuffed under there."

Vanessa let me cough for a moment before she said, "I used some of it, remember? And then I put it in the cupboard.

"Thanks for telling me," I grumbled. I dragged myself back out from under the bed and opened the cupboard door. Sure enough, the poster board was there, along with my plastic case full of Magic Markers.

"What are you making?" Vanessa asked, as I cut the board in half.

"You'll see." I wrote carefully in big, bold black letters. Then I found my red clip-on braces and, attaching them to each poster board, looped them over my head. Finally I faced Vanessa, who read my sign out loud.

"'Mallory on Strike.'"

"You got it!" I said triumphantly. I marched out of the bedroom and made my way downstairs. It was time to break the news to the rest of my family.

"Look at Mallory!" Claire cried as I marched into the dining room. She pointed a sticky finger at me.

My father lowered the newspaper he was reading just enough to peer over the top. "That's a sandwich board," he said.

Byron read the sign out loud. "'Mallory on Strike.' What's that mean?"

I slid into my place at the table. Luckily, the poster board was flexible, so I could sit down. "It means that I'm not going to pick up any toys, settle any fights over music, or find any lost pets today."

"What's going on?" my mum asked. She put a bowl of fried potatoes on the table.

Claire licked one gooey finger and said, "Mallory's not going to play with us today."

I spooned some potatoes onto my plate and said, "I'm striking."

"You mean, like in baseball?" Nicky asked. "Three strikes, and you're out?"

"Sort of. Only this is *one* strike, and *I'm* out."

"Out of what?" Jordan demanded.

"Patience," I muttered under my breath, then quickly added, "out of commission. I'm going to be in my room and I don't want anyone to disturb me."

"You have to stay in your room?" Margo asked.

"I don't *have* to," I corrected her. "I *want* to."

"You want to?" Claire's eyes grew wide. "That's awful."

It was clear that my brothers and sisters had no idea what 'on strike' meant. "People go on strike when they want their working conditions to change," I explained, "or when they want higher wages."

Jordan squinted one eye shut. "You mean, like more pocket money?"

I nodded. "Yes."

"All right!" Jordan folded his arms across his chest. "Then I'm on strike, too."

"Now, hold on a minute," my father called from behind his paper. "Only one Pike child at a time can go on strike."

"After breakfast I'm going to my room," I announced, "and I don't want anyone to talk to me, or ask me questions, or call me to the phone, or even touch my door."

"You want to be alone," my father said, folding up the paper and placing it beside his plate. "I think we get the picture."

"Good." I took a sip of milk and smiled at my father. He really seemed to understand.

Margo, who had been watching me closely, suddenly shook her head. "Not fair. Mal gets to sit in her room all day and get more pocket money."

I listened to my brothers and sisters talk and wondered if it were possible for an entire family to have a screw loose. It certainly sounded like it from their conversation.

I hurried through breakfast, then excused myself from the table, saying pointedly, "I'll see everyone tonight."

"Poor Mallory," I heard Claire murmur as I left the room. "She's on strike. No cartoons, no toys, no fun."

Once I was in my room (and Vanessa was out), I sat down at my desk and started to write. Several times I heard footsteps and whispering outside my door, but everyone respected my wishes.

I worked on my story for hours, fine-tuning every word. It was wonderful. At last I felt like a real writer.

## 12th CHAPTER

Saturday

I must admit, it was weird getting a call from the Pikes wanting us to babysit in one hour.

Dawn said "us" because they wanted two sitters. Which was doubly bizarre. We wondered where Mal was.

She had told us she'd be home all afternoon. Mary Anne and I figured something strange must have happened, and Mal's plans had changed.

So we spent an action-packed afternoon with the Pike kids.

And we found out what happened to Mal. The hard way...

I had no idea that my parents were going out or that they had phoned Mary Anne and Dawn to baby-sit. And, I was so busy concentrating on my story that I didn't hear the doorbell ring.

"Do you think something awful has happened to Mal?" Mary Anne asked Dawn, as they waited for someone to answer the door.

"I don't think so." Dawn flipped a strand of her long, blonde hair over her shoulder. "Mrs Pike would have said something."

My father opened the door then. "Hi, girls! Thanks for coming at such short notice. Mrs Pike and I got a call from the Stoneybrook Library. They've scheduled an emergency board meeting."

"I hope nothing terrible has happened to the library," Mary Anne said, as she stepped inside the house.

"Oh, it hasn't burned down or anything like that," my father assured her, as he slipped on his coat. "We think they may be in some sort of financial trouble."

Mary Anne and Dawn nodded sympathetically. They didn't know what to say. It's hard to understand how a library operates, or where it gets its money, or any of that complicated stuff.

"Mallory is up in her room," my father said.

"She's here?" Dawn gasped. "You mean, you need *three* sitters?"

My father chuckled. "No, no. Mallory's working on her story in her room and asked that she not be disturbed, which is why Mrs Pike suggested I call you."

My mother hurried out of the kitchen, tucking a packet of tissues into her bag. She thanked Dawn and Mary Anne for coming to help, then handed them a sheet of paper.

"This is where we'll be for the next two hours," she explained. "There's pizza, orange juice, and fruit in the fridge." She ticked off her list of reminders on her fingers. "The boys know they can't bring their bow and arrow set into the house. Margo has been given strict instructions not to play with my make-up. Vanessa has a slight cold and should stay quiet, if possible."

"How do you remember all that?" Dawn asked in amazement.

My mother slipped a scarf over her head and sighed. "Practice."

Just as my parents were going out of the door, my mother called, "One more thing. The kids told me to tell you two that you're *it*."

She shut the door behind her and Dawn turned to Mary Anne. "We're *it*?"

Mary Anne nodded. "The kids must be hiding."

She was answered by a flurry of giggles from the living room.

"I was wondering where everybody was," Dawn said, tiptoeing out of the hall. Then she sang in a high, mysterious voice, "Come out, come out, wherever you are."

More giggles answered Dawn, who pointed towards the sofa. Mary Anne nodded, then pointed to the cupboard. "I wonder if they've all run away from home."

"Maybe they were kidnapped," Dawn said loudly.

"I hope not," Mary Anne replied, putting her hand on the cupboard door. "Then we'd be all alone and have to eat that pizza by ourselves."

She pulled open the cupboard door just as Dawn looked behind the sofa. Both girls shouted, "Gotcha!"

They were answered by shrill war whoops from the triplets, who sprang out of the cupboard, wearing feathered headbands. Nicky and Margo leaped from behind the sofa, waving cowboy hats.

"*Aieee!*" Adam bellowed. "You're our prisoners!"

"No, they're *our* prisoners," Nicky said, wrapping his arms round Mary Anne's knees.

"But we were here first," Byron said, grabbing Dawn's wrist.

110

"Were not," Nicky shouted.

"Were too!" Jordan grabbed Dawn by the other wrist.

Mary Anne clapped her hands above her head. "You were both here at exactly the same moment."

Margo looped an imaginary rope around Dawn and Mary Anne. "Then you're *all* of our prisoners."

"Yeah!" the boys cried, patting their hands on their mouths and hopping around in a circle like cartoon Indians. Vanessa wandered in during their war dance and settled into an armchair with a book.

"Let's throw them in the dungeon!" Jordan said, folding his arms across his chest.

"Oh, no!" Mary Anne cried, playing along with their game. "Please don't do that. It would hurt."

Nicky scratched his head. "Then let's freeze 'em."

"Freeze 'em?" Vanessa commented from her chair in the corner. "Nobody freezes prisoners."

"Do, too." Nicky put his hand on his hips and glared at his sister.

"They do not," Vanessa answered stubbornly.

"Wanna bet?"

"Okay, I'll bet you a million dollars."

"Hold it," Mary Anne ordered. "I think we have a small problem."

The kids stopped arguing and turned their attention to Mary Anne, who asked Dawn, "How many Pikes do you count?"

Dawn spun slowly in a circle as she counted. "Six."

"And how many are we supposed to be watching today?" Mary Anne asked.

"Seven." Dawn's blue eyes widened. "Oh, no! We've lost—" She glanced quickly around the room. "Claire."

This was especially upsetting since Claire is the youngest of all my sisters and brothers and needs looking after the most.

"Okay, everyone," Mary Anne ordered. "Spread out and find Claire. The second you do, bring her back to the kitchen."

"Do we get a reward?" Nicky asked.

Dawn and Mary Anne exchanged looks. Finally Dawn said, "Yes. Pizza."

"Oh, boy!" Byron whooped. "Let's go." He ran out of the room with the other triplets following him.

"I'll look in the bedrooms," Margo said, racing for the stairs.

"Fine," Dawn said. "But keep out of your mother's make-up, okay?"

Margo hesitated, then puffed out her lower lip. "Okay."

Vanessa put down her book and got up from her chair. "I'll check out the back."

"I'll look out the front," Mary Anne said,

"and Dawn, you wait here in case one of the other kids finds her."

"I'll go with you," Nicky said, tucking his hand in Mary Anne's.

Dawn kept telling herself not to get nervous. The kids had been playing a game of hide-and-seek; maybe Claire was still hiding. Then again, maybe she wasn't. Dawn peered into the kitchen. No sign of Claire. She was just about to go upstairs when she heard a piping sound, like singing. She stopped and listened. The sound was coming from the stairs leading down to the TV room.

"*Playmates, come out and play with me, and bring your dollies three, dee dee dee dee dee dee,*" a high, little voice sang, slightly off-key.

Dawn peered round the corner. Sitting on the top step was Claire, holding two clothes-pegs in her hand. She danced them on her leg as if they were dolls.

"Hello, there," Dawn said gently. "Who are your playmates?"

Claire held up the clothes-pegs. "This is Tilly and this is Milly."

"What are their last names?" Dawn asked.

"Silly-billy-goo-goo."

"Would you like to invite Tilly and Milly for a snack? We're having pizza."

"That's their favourite," Claire declared

with a grin. She got up and followed Dawn into the kitchen.

Dawn remembered that Mary Anne and the rest of the Pikes were still on their search-and-rescue mission, so she called out of the front door, "It's okay! I've found her."

Mary Anne relayed the message to the back garden. Then, after removing four pairs of muddy shoes (the kids had all found the one mud puddle and made sure they jumped in it), she led Nicky and the triplets into the kitchen for pizza.

Heating frozen pizza sounds like a simple task, but it isn't. Not when you're feeding the Pike family. Dawn had to remove the pepperoni for Jordan and the onions for Nicky, while Mary Anne trimmed the crust off for Margo and made sure that Claire's slice was cut into bite-sized pieces. Finally Mary Anne and Dawn leaned back in their chairs, exhausted, and watched the kids eat.

"When I have children," Dawn declared, "I'm having one boy and one girl. That's it."

"Me, too," Mary Anne agreed. "I don't know how Mr and Mrs Pike do it."

After lunch, the kids put their plates in the dishwasher, then Dawn suggested they play Snakes & Ladders. While they formed a circle on the living room carpet, Mary

Anne cleaned off the work surface and made sure the kitchen was sparkling clean. After she was finished, she thought she'd go upstairs to see how I was doing. Big mistake.

The knock on the door came as such a shock that I bellowed, "*Whaaaat*?" at the top of my lungs. It sounded as if I had been interrupted all day, but this was the first time. (Even Vanessa hadn't ventured into the bedroom, and half of it is hers.)

Mary Anne sprang backwards when she heard the sharp tone in my voice. "Mal?" she said timidly. "It's me, Mary Anne."

"Mary Anne?" I pushed back my chair. "What are you doing here? Come on in."

Mary Anne opened the door but didn't step into the room. She just stuck her head around the jamb and said, "Sorry to disturb you, Mal, but Dawn and I are babysitting downstairs and I thought I'd say hi and see how you're doing."

"Babysitting?" That was news to me.

Mary Anne explained about the emergency meeting. "I suppose your parents didn't want to bother you," she said. "So they phoned Dawn and me."

"Gee." I blinked in surprise. "I didn't know anything about that. That was really nice of them."

Mary Anne stepped just inside the door, as if she thought I might snap at her again. "I'm glad you talked things over with your parents. It must have made you feel a lot better."

I looked at my "Mallory on Strike" sign leaning against the bed and suddenly felt a bit ashamed. "I haven't talked to them at all," I admitted. "I woke up this morning and decided to go on strike. I made that sign and told my parents that I had to write and I didn't want any interruptions."

Mary Anne crossed the room and sat on my bed. "You mean, as soon as your story is finished, things will go back to the way they were before?"

She had a point. Finding the time to work on my story had become a problem mostly because of the demands my parents made of me. They automatically assumed that I would be available to help with house-cleaning, food-making, babysitting, or running errands day and night.

Mary Anne leaned forward. "Mal, I think you need to have a good heart-to-heart with your parents as soon as they get home. They're great people, and I'm sure they'll understand how frustrated you're feeling. If you like, Dawn and I will look after the kids while you do it."

I took Mary Anne's advice and, boy, was I glad I did! As soon as my parents got home, I asked if I could talk to them in my room. Then, for the next fifteen minutes, I poured my heart out.

"It's not that I don't love all of you," I said, finishing my speech, "but sometimes I need time to myself."

Mum and Dad looked at each other for a moment.

"Mallory, we're so proud of the work you do at school," my mother said, "and the way you help out at home, and how you're such a responsible babysitter. I think sometimes we forget to show it."

"And you're right," my father added, giving me a big hug. "We do take advantage of you sometimes. We're sorry and we'll try not to do it again." Then he smiled. "At least, not too often."

"You know what I think you need?" my mother said, kissing me on the forehead. "I think you need a special day, just for you."

"What do you mean?" I asked.

"You need a day off," she explained. "One that's just for you, without having to worry about looking after the kids, or helping your father and me."

"Gosh." I tried to imagine how that would feel. "I think I'd like that."

"Just choose the day," my father said, pointing to the calendar pinned to my notice board. "And it's yours."

It didn't take me long to decide on a day. I had almost finished my story and I felt really good about it, so I blurted out, "How about tomorrow?"

"Tomorrow it is!" My father put one arm around my mother and one arm around me and said, "I hereby declare tomorrow to be Mallory Pike Day!"

It's hard to describe what was going on inside me then. My feelings were so topsy-turvy, I didn't know whether to laugh or cry. So I did both.

# 13th CHAPTER

Sunday. My special day. I couldn't wait to get started. I was so excited that I changed my clothes three times before finally settling on my denim skirt and jacket, bright red tights, trainers, and multi-coloured earrings that Claud had made for me.

Mum and Dad said I could do anything I wanted for the whole day. I wanted to go to Washington Shopping City. And I wanted to take Jessi too. After all, a special day wouldn't be special without my best friend to share it with.

My parents asked Mary Anne and Dawn to babysit again, and luckily they were available. After a frenzied half hour getting my brothers and sisters dressed and making sure they'd eaten breakfast and put their dishes in the dishwasher, we were finally ready to go.

Waving goodbye to my brothers and sisters and getting into the car with Mum and Dad felt sort of strange. For the first time in my life, I felt as if I belonged with the grown-ups. For a while I had the back seat all to myself, which was also weird. (Of course, that didn't last for very long because we made one stop before we headed for the shopping arcade.)

"Jessi!"

She met me on her front porch, dressed in a new purple outfit with a gold polo-neck, which made her look taller and more like a dancer than ever.

"I'm so excited!" Jessi said, as we hurried back to the car. "I've raided my piggy bank just for today and I'm planning to do some major shopping."

"Me, too!" I giggled. "Let's get going."

Washington Shopping City is about a half-hour ride from Stoneybrook. It has five levels and is the biggest one in our part of Connecticut. I mean, it is huge! If I had an entire special weekend, I don't think I'd be able to get to every shop in it. But Jessi and I were going to do our best.

"You girls have a great time," Mum said, as my parents dropped us off at the big front entrance. "We'll meet you at midday for lunch."

"Where?" I asked, waiting for my mother to give me her usual instructions. But this time was different.

120

"It's your day," she said with a smile. "You choose the place."

Jessi and I looked at each other and blurted out at the same time, "Casa Grande!"

We love Mexican food, particularly when it's covered with sour cream and guacamole. Like the Super Burrito at Casa Grande.

"Casa Grande it is," my dad said. "See you in two hours."

The arcade was crowded with kids. I grabbed Jessi's hand and made a beeline for Stuff 'n' Nonsense, one of my favourite shops. On the way, we passed the ear-piercing boutique (where Jessi and I had *finally* got ours pierced), and I started giggling.

"What's so funny?" Jessi asked.

"I was just thinking about the time I took Margo and Claire to watch a girl getting her ears pierced. When the woman squeezed the trigger on the ear-piercing gun, Claire screamed as though she'd been shot. Then Margo announced to everyone within a hundred-mile radius that she was going to throw up!"

Jessi laughed, too. "I wonder if those two will ever get their ears pierced?"

"Margo might. She likes putting on make-up and playing dressing up. But Claire thinks it's too painful-looking." A pair of tiny pink bow earrings in a shop's window display caught my eye, and I added, "Although I bet she'd think those were really cute."

Just thinking about my sisters at home made me feel a little funny inside. Almost sad. I know they would have loved a trip to the arcade.

As Jessi and I walked through the main concourse, we could hear music pounding from one of the centre stalls. A small crowd was gathered around a stage where a pudgy boy was playing an electronic keyboard. A tall guy stood nearby at a microphone. In front of them was a cute blond boy demonstrating what looked like a board balanced on a ball.

"Look, Jessi." I pulled her to the front of the crowd. "It's like a skateboard. Boy, Nicky would practically pass out if he saw this."

Jessi nudged me with her elbow. "Listen, they're going to sing."

The tall guy took the microphone off its stand and dropped automatically to one knee, as if he were going to sing something really great. Instead, this is what came out: "*The Teeter Streeter is really cool; you can play with it at home, or take it to school.*"

"Teeter Streeter?" Jessi and I repeated, then burst out laughing. The singer heard us and gave us a dirty look, which made Jessi laugh even harder.

"Cut it out," I said, poking her in the ribs. "He's staring at us."

"I can't help it," she gasped. "Teeter Streeter is such a dorky name."

As the singer shouted, "*You can hop, you can bop on the Teeter Streeter*," the boy demonstrating the toy performed a few dance moves in response to the lyrics. Then he fell to his knees as the singer crooned, "*Do the flop and drop, no, it couldn't be sweeter*."

Jessi was laughing so hard, she gave herself the hiccups. I hustled her along the concourse away from the stage. She stopped hiccupping as soon as we were out of sight of the band. But from then on, every few minutes one of us would sing, "*The Teeter Streeter is really cool*," and then the other would make up a silly rhyme, like, "You'll look like a geek and act like a fool." Then we would start giggling all over again.

We finally reached Stuff 'n' Nonsense and headed straight for the earrings. "I've always wanted little pearl studs," I said, twirling the rack.

"Giraffes and elephants!" Jessi cried in delight. She held up tiny carved animals that dangled on a gold hoop. "These are so cute."

I hurried to her side and found a pair of pink flamingos that I thought were adorable. "Should we both get animal earrings?" I asked, holding them up to my ear and studying my reflection in the mirror.

"Yes!" Jessi cried.

We asked the saleswoman to ring up our purchases before we could change our minds. She handed us each a bright pink bag, and we moved on to the next shop, which was called Eastern Standard. An hour flew by as we tried on sweaters and jeans and skirts. Jessi finally settled on a sweater, and I found a checked waistcoat I liked. I have to admit, splurging on myself was fun. But it was time to put a stop to it. I was quickly running out of my hard-earned babysitting money.

"Where should we go next?" Jessi asked as we left the shop.

I looked up and down the concourse. It almost made me dizzy. Record shops, restaurants, shoes shops, sweet shops, card shops—you name it, Washington Shopping City has it. A shop caught my eye on the next level.

"Let's check out Zingy's," I said.

Zingy's is this really cool place that sells punk clothing. Not only are the clothes outrageous but the salespeople are bizarre. The boy who greeted us at the door was no exception. His black hair was dyed bright red on top, and a peace symbol had been shaved into the side of his head.

"Anything I can help you with?" he

asked, resting a foot on the bumper of a bright red convertible that sat in the centre of the shop. (It wasn't a whole car, just the front of one.)

I was feeling pretty silly, so I said, "My friend is looking for some leather boots. The really clunky kind."

"No problem." He motioned for us to follow him towards the back of the shop.

"What?" Jessi exclaimed.

I put my finger to my lips and shushed her.

"Look at those!" I pointed to a pair of heavy black leather work boots with metal-tipped toes. "They must weigh a ton."

"Nah, they just look that way," the fellow answered.

"My friend would like to try on a pair," I said with a straight face. "Size six."

The salesman disappeared behind a fake brick wall, and Jessi turned to me and hissed, "Mal, what are you doing? I don't want any boots."

"I know you don't," I said. "But I've always wondered what those shoes feel like."

"Then why don't *you* try them on?"

I was about to answer when my eye caught sight of the giant alarm clock hanging over the cash register. It said five minutes to twelve.

"Oh, no!" I shouted. "We've only got

125

five minutes to get to Casa Grande and it's way up on the fifth level."

"What about the shoes?" Jessi asked, as I pulled her by the arm towards the front of the store.

"We'll come back another time," I replied. "Maybe . . ."

We raced for the escalators and rode up to the fifth floor, the food circus, which was brightly decorated with mirrors and neon lights. My parents were waiting patiently by the Mexican food restaurant.

"It looks like you bought out the arcade," my father remarked, smiling at the shopping bags we were hauling along.

"Yeah, it's a good thing it's lunchtime," Jessi said, "or we'd be broke."

While we ate our burritos, I told my parents all about our adventure at Zingy's and the Teeter Streeter demonstration, which gave Jessi and me the giggles all over again. I was sipping my Coke when I started laughing and the soda fizzed up my nose and everybody laughed.

"That's something Jordan would do," my mother said as she handed me a paper napkin.

"You know, I feel really strange being here without everyone else," I said as I dabbed at my chin. "First, I found these cute earrings that I know Margo would just love. And then when we walked by the bookshop window, I saw this display of

126

Emily Dickinson's poems and I thought about Vanessa. Do you think she'd like a copy of an Emily Dickinson book?"

My mother smiled, "I'm sure she would."

I took the final bite of my burrito and a (careful) sip of my Coke. "I've got a bit of money left. Maybe I'll get it for her. As a gift for surviving my grumpiness."

I saw the look on Jessi's face and added, "I know, I know. I should probably give everyone a present since I've been such a grouch lately." Then a light went on in my head. "Hey, that gives me an idea!"

"What?" Jessi asked as we followed my parents out of Casa Grande and towards the escalators.

"I need to think about it a little more," I replied. "I'll tell you tonight."

I did think about it, all the way back to Stoneybrook. And all the way through the film we went to, and even while we were eating triple-decker sundaes at the ice cream parlour afterwards. I realized that having my own special day was truly wonderful, but something important was missing. The rest of my family.

I know Margo and Claire would have liked to look at Zoo Animals, the toy shop, and Nicky would have loved watching the Teeter Streeter demonstration, and the triplets would have had a blast at the video arcade. I realized that life may get pretty

127

crazy doing things with ten people, but it's always different and fun.

My parents dropped Jessi off at her house.

When we got home, Mary Anne (who looked a little frazzled) met us at the door. She was surrounded by my brothers and sisters.

"How was your day?" I asked.

"Interesting," was all she said.

Dawn, looking a little glassy-eyed, added, "And loud."

I giggled. After Dawn and Mary Anne left, I gathered my brothers and sisters in the living room and told them I wanted to make an announcement. Claire crawled onto my lap. Nicky stood behind me on the couch, resting his elbows on my shoulders. The triplets sat cross-legged in front of me, and Vanessa and Margo knelt beside the boys.

"I had a great time today," I began. "But something was missing."

"Your mittens?" Claire suggested helpfully. She's always losing hers.

"No." I gave her a squeeze. "What I missed was all of you."

A funny look crossed Jordan's face. "Us?"

"Really?" Byron asked.

"Yup."

"We missed you, too!" Nicky said, resting his chin on top of my head.

I took a deep breath and said, "So I've planned a surprise for you—"

"What is it?" Margo said, bouncing up and down. "Tell me, tell me, please!"

I ruffled her hair playfully. "If I told you, it wouldn't be a surprise. Just trust me that it will be lots of fun."

"When's the surprise going to happen?" Adam asked.

"I can't tell you that, either," I said in my most mysterious voice. "Just know that it will happen . . ." I paused, then whispered, "soon!"

# 14th CHAPTER

Young Authors Day. At last! I woke up on Saturday morning feeling tingly. I was excited, scared, nervous, and happy all at once.

My story, "Caught in the Middle," was lying on a display table at Stoneybrook Middle School. In just a few hours I would find out what the judges thought of it. After four weeks of hard work and frustration, I would finally find out who was the sixth-grade's best overall fiction writer. Believe me, it was agony not knowing. As I dressed, I made myself concentrate on something besides the competition. Mr Dougherty had planned a day of exciting activities, so I tried to keep my mind on them.

Getting dressed and eating breakfast was just a blur. About the only part of me working normally was my mouth. By the time my family piled into our estate car to drive to the school, I was chattering away non-stop.

"Pamme Reed, the author of *Bradley and the Great Chase*, is going to talk to the assembly first," I announced to anyone who'd listen.

Margo and Nicky were pinching each other, and the triplets were making faces at some kids in the car driving next to us, but Vanessa and my parents seemed to be paying attention.

"After that comes the awards portion of the programme." (My voice wobbled a bit when I said that. I hoped nobody noticed.) "After that, people can look at all the entries on display, while some of us attend the afternoon workshops." (I had signed up for both of them.) "Then Pamme Reed will be autographing her books in the library. Isn't that exciting?" I had brought along my copy of her newest book for her to sign.

"Look, it's Jessi!" Nicky shouted as my father pulled into the school car park. She was standing on the kerb, waiting for me.

"Let me out of here, Dad," I called over the shouts of hello from my brothers and sisters. Dad brought the car to a stop and I opened the door. Jessi ran to me.

"Mal, the assembly hall is packed!" she reported. "Every kid at school must've brought their whole family!"

That wasn't exactly what I needed to hear. "Great!" I said, trying to keep my voice steady. "Mr D. will be thrilled."

"I saved seats for us in the front row." Jessi grabbed my arm. "Come on!"

"We'll find a place at the back so that we can watch you get your award," my mother called from the car.

"Go get 'em, sweetheart!" my father added.

Boy, I wished I felt half as confident as my parents sounded. When we reached the assembley hall, I realized Jessi hadn't been exaggerating. (I almost turned round and ran.) As Jessi and I made our way down the aisle, several kids said hi to me, but I was too nervous to stop and chat.

The lights dimmed a few minutes after we'd taken our seats. A couple of boys cheered and whistled. (One of them was probably Benny Ott. He can be such a show-off.) Then our head teacher walked onto the stage, followed by Mr Dougherty and the rest of the English teachers at school. They sat down in a row of chairs behind the head teacher, Mr Taylor, who stood at the podium.

"Welcome to Young Authors Day," Mr Taylor announced, and everyone applauded. I slumped down in my seat and tried to stop my heart from pounding. It felt as if it was going to jump out of my chest.

Mr Taylor made some general welcoming

statements, and the next thing I knew, Mr Dougherty was at the podium. "I have been given the great privilege of introducing our guest speaker," he said. "She has received many awards for her work in children's literature. I would like to say that besides being a terrific writer, Pamme Reed is also a wonderful person."

"It sounds as if Mr Dougherty knows her personally," Jessi whispered into my ear.

"I bet he does," I said proudly. "He's a very good writer himself." I beamed up at my teacher and tried to imagine how it would feel to be a famous writer and be introduced in such glowing terms.

"So without further ado," Mr Dougherty continued, "let's give a big hand for Ms Pamme Reed!"

Everyone cheered this time, and a few more boys whistled. (This time I was certain the loudest one was Benny Ott.) Then the famous writer stepped onto the stage from the wings.

Pamme Reed looked like an artist in her Indian-print skirt, suede waistcoat, white blouse with puffed sleeves, and sleek boots. She had shoulder-length red hair, which fell about her shoulders in thick, beautiful waves. I decided then and there that, if by some miracle I survived the next half hour and didn't keel over from nerves, I would try to look and dress like Pamme Reed.

I have to admit it was hard for me to concentrate on her speech. Ms Reed was saying some really interesting things about writing and about how she first got published, but all I could think about was my story and the awards ceremony.

"How are you doing?" Jessi whispered halfway through Ms Reed's speech.

"Fine," I murmured back. "Why?"

"Um . . . you look a bit tense." She pointed to my hands, which were folded in my lap. I was gripping them so hard that my knuckles had turned white. I tried to force myself to take a deep breath and relax. It didn't work.

Ms Reed finished her speech by encouraging us to keep writing. "I look forward to talking to you this afternoon at the book signing," she added.

We applauded loudly as she sat down beside Mr Dougherty. Then Mr Taylor introduced Hand Jive, a puppet group from New York City. The group presented a short show about how reading can stimulate the imagination. I think I may have laughed harder than some of the other kids because I was so nervous, but the show really was funny.

When the show had finished, Mr Dougherty stepped up to the podium once more. He unfolded a piece of paper and adjusted his glasses, while a couple of the teachers put a small table beside him. Some rolled-up papers tied with ribbons were piled on the table. Jessi took hold of my hand and squeezed it hard. "This is it, Mal."

I could only nod and stare straight ahead. Mr Dougherty started by announcing the winners from selected catagories, like Best Poem, Best Illustration, Best Science Fiction Story, and Best Short Play. Each winner ran down the aisle right beside me and climbed the stairs to the stage. The girl who won Best Mystery tripped going up and almost fell on her face. Some people laughed, and I was seized with a new fear. What if I won and then embarrassed myself by doing the same thing?

Finally, after what seemed like an eternity, Mr Dougherty announced the category of Best Overall Fiction for the Sixth Grade. He smiled at the assembled students. "It was particularly difficult to pick a winner for this category," he said. "The judges said they received quite a few excellent stories."

"Uh-oh," I mumbled, sliding down in my seat again. Jessi was still clutching my hand, but I could no longer bear to watch Mr Dougherty. I squeezed my eyes shut and forced myself to listen to the rest of his speech.

"All of us agreed that the stories were very original and quite well written," Mr Dougherty continued. "But one story seemed to stand out above the others—"

My heart was pounding so hard it sounded like a freight train in my ears. My stomach did flip-flops as I thought about Rebecca Mason, one of the girls in my creative writing class. She had handed in her story early, and then sat around all week looking smug while the rest of us frantically tried to get ours finished in time. Her cover looked as though it had been done by a professional illustrator. I had been the last pupil in my class to hand in a story. And my cover looked really homemade next to hers.

Suddenly it came to me like a flash. Of course! Rebecca was going to win. How could I even think I had a chance?

Mr Dougherty was still talking, but his words sounded like a tape being played too slowly and I could barely understand him.

"That story was written by—"

I heard thunderous applause and I tried to put on a congratulatory face for Rebecca Mason. I turned in my seat, with a forced smile on my face, and watched for her to come down the aisle.

But no one was there. And suddenly Jessi threw her arms around my neck.

"You did it!" she squealed. "You did it!"

"I did?" I blinked uncomprehendingly at my friend. "Are you sure?"

"Yes!"

I didn't know what to say. I just sat in my seat, unable to move. It was really strange. For four weeks all I could think about was winning the award for Best Overall Fiction for the Sixth Grade, and now that I had won it, I was numb with shock.

"Hurry up," Jessi urged me. "Go and get your award."

She practically had to push me out of my seat and point me towards the stage.

I stumbled up the steps, unaware of what my feet were doing. Then Mr Taylor shook my hand, and Pamme Reed handed me the certificate herself. Mr Dougherty was smiling from ear to ear. He leant down and whispered, "I knew you could do it, Mallory! You're a real writer now."

I think hearing that was as great as winning the prize.

"Thank you." I turned to look at the crowd in the assembly hall. Little flashes of light were popping like fireworks as people took pictures. My family was standing near the back with all my friends, cheering and waving. Even Benny Ott and several of his pals were clapping their hands above their heads and whistling. (Maybe Benny's not so bad after all.)

I was grinning so hard that my face hurt. I felt the way those women look when they win the Miss America beauty contest. You know, when they're smiling, and their faces are shining, but tears are streaming down their cheeks? I think I'll remember that moment for as long as I live.

Jessi met me on the other side of the stage, and the two of us raced up the aisle to show my family the award. Dad took about a hundred pictures of me with my certificate.

Then it was time for the workshops, which were really interesting. The first was called, "A Picture Is Worth a Thousand Words." It was led by an illustrator who showed us how words and drawings can make a story progress.

The second workshop was about what happens to a book when it is published. I never dreamed how many steps a book had to go through before it got to me. The woman giving the workshop, who's an editor at a big publishing company in New York City, told us it usually takes a *year* from the time an author sells the book to a publisher until it ends up in bookshops.

While we were in the workshops, the school had opened the cafeteria, where the work of every pupil who participated in Young Authors Day was on display. The stories ranged in length from just a few pages to a short novel. All of them had brightly coloured covers. The judges had given many of the booklets blue stickers for honourable mention. There were red stickers for third-place winners, silver stickers for second-place, and beautiful shiny gold stickers for the first-place winners.

My family found my book displayed on a far table by the window. "Look," my sister Vanessa cried, when I joined them later. "I think thousands of people have already read your story."

"Vanessa, there aren't a thousand people here," I said. But I was glowing inside because the book really did look as if a lot of people had read it.

The day ended perfectly. First, Pamme Reed autographed my copy of her new book and then wrote a note of congratulation on my story. She wished me luck in my career as a writer. We talked about how difficult it is to find just the right words to fit your thoughts and feelings. She treated me as if I was a real author!

When the day was over, and my family was back at home, I gathered my brothers and sisters in the living room and said, "It's time for me to tell you about my surprise."

"Oh, goody!" cried Claire.

"I've had my special day," I said, "and it was wonderful, but next weekend, Jessi and I are going to take *you* out for your very own special day!"

"Our own day?" Margo repeated.

"Yes. And it's going to be packed with

fun things to do. I want each of you to dress in clothes you might wear if you were an explorer."

"You mean, like jeans and stuff?" Jordan asked.

"Right. You never know what kind of terrain we'll be covering. Wear a jacket and comfortable shoes. Also I want you each to carry a rucksack."

"What should we put in our rucksack?" Claire asked.

"A newspaper, a paper bag, and something you can make music with."

"Like what?" Margo asked.

I smiled mysteriously. "Use your imagination."

# 15th
# CHAPTER

*"Exploring we will go! Exploring we will go! Hi, ho, the derry-oh, exploring we will go!"*

Jessi and I led my seven brothers and sisters down the pavement in front of our house, singing at the tops of our voices. In fact, we were so loud that some of the neighbours peered out of their front doors to see what the racket was. But as soon as they recognized us, marching in single file down the street like a band of explorers, they smiled and ducked back inside their houses.

I suppose it was my fault that we were making so much noise, but I couldn't help it. I felt wonderful. I had just spent one of the best weeks of my life. For five whole days, teachers and kids, some of whom I'd never met before, stopped me in the corridors at school to congratulate me on my award. Mr Dougherty even asked the

141

writing class to give me a special round of applause when I entered the classroom. But, best of all, I was back in the BSC.

"We certainly missed you, Mal," Kristy said, when I arrived for the Monday meeting at Claud's house.

"I missed you lot, too." I sat down in my old spot on the floor next to Jessi. "And I want to apologize to everyone for being such a grouch. I suppose I was a little touchy there for a while."

"Don't ever let it happen again," Kristy teased, shaking her finger at me sternly, "or we'll make you stand on your head and eat live worms—"

"Or roasted eels," Dawn said, looking at Claud. "From Maurice's."

"Ugh, ugh, ugh, ugh!" Claudia cried, squinching up her nose.

We all began describing the most disgusting things we could think of to eat. Within minutes we were laughing so hard, tears were streaming down our cheeks. Then the phone rang and we fell back into our comfortable routine. I leaned against the bed and smiled at my friends, just happy to be back in the club.

Things may have been the same with the BSC, but they had certainly changed at home. After my talk with Mum and Dad, they got together and decided that from now on, if I needed private time for my homework or my writing, I could use the desk in their bedroom. Can you believe it? On top of that, they said I could put a *Do Not Disturb* sign on the doorknob while I'm working, and that everyone has to honour it. Dad made the official announcement to the family at dinner on Monday. "Whenever that sign is out, *no one* is to bother Mallory."

Then my mum said that, of course, she and Dad will still expect me to help out with my brothers and sisters and do chores around the house, but they'll only ask for big favours if I'm free. That means that if I have another writing project and really need some private time, I can have it. Isn't that great?

Not being forced to take care of my brothers and sisters made me appreciate them a whole lot more. That's why I was looking forward so much to our special day together.

Jessi and I spent the week thinking up fun activities. I'll admit, we were as excited as the kids were.

On Saturday morning, Jessi met me at our door at seven o'clock. She was armed with a sack full of art supplies, including a pack of Magic Markers, and some special treats of her own. We hurried to the park to prepare it for our outing and then rushed back to the house. We had been gone just over an hour and when we got back, all seven of my brothers and sisters met us at the door. They were dressed in jeans, sweat shirts, and jackets, as I'd instructed.

"I'm glad you two came back," my mum called from the kitchen. "They've been standing like this for fifteen minutes, waiting for you to return."

I had found an old police whistle on a leather cord in the garage, and had hung it around my neck. I was also wearing a visor like Kristy's. I thought that would make me seem more like a leader. I blew on the whistle, then announced, "Good morning, Explorers. Are you ready for the big day?"

"Yes!" The triplets shouted so loudly that Margo and Claire covered their ears. But they were grinning.

"All right, then." I pointed towards the stairs. "Our first stop is the TV room, where you will make your uniforms."

The kids ran for the stairs so fast that for a second I was afraid we might start off the day with a sprained ankle or a bump on the head.

Jessi took charge once we were all downstairs. She held up her newspaper. "All right, Explorers," she cried. "It's time to make your official Explorer Hats!"

"Oh, boy, oh, boy!" Nicky shouted gleefully. (The kids were so excited that everything they said seemed to come out at full volume.)

As I helped them fold their hats, I said, "And for today, you can each choose a special name for yourself, because today is all about make-believe."

Nicky chose Frodo, after our pet hamster. The triplets named themselves Robin Hood, Little John, and Friar Tuck. Vanessa decided to be Emily Dickinson. (She loved the book I'd bought her at the arcade!) Margo decided to be Queen Margo.

Finally Claire, who had been quietly wrestling with her hat, held it up to me. "Write my name, please."

"What do you want to be called?" I asked.

"Mallory." She gave me a big grin.

I was surprised. "Not 'Mean Old Mallory'?"

She giggled and shook her head so hard her hair bounced. "Nope. Just Mallory."

My vision grew blurry and I knelt beside my little sister and squeezed her so hard she cried, "Ow!"

"Everybody ready?" Jessi asked.

"Yes!" came the resounding chorus.

Jessi and I led our explorers out of the door and down the street.

First stop was the circus that a lot of kids were putting on in the Braddocks' back garden. I pulled out my change purse and handed each of my brothers and sisters the admission fee—one nickel.

"Oh, goody," Claire cried. "A circus."

The circus was a short event. It featured Buddy Barrett as Jocko the Lion Tamer and

Pow, his dog, as the Lion. Matt Braddock played Thor the Strong Man, who lifted a broomstick with balloons tied to either end. That act was short-lived because Byron sat on one end of the pretend barbells and popped the balloons. The finale of the show was performed by Suzi Barrett, who demonstrated the latest moves she'd learned in gym class.

Even though it was a pretty small circus, my brothers and sisters applauded as loudly as if they were watching the greatest show on earth. When it was over, Jessi, who had made prior arrangements with Mrs Braddock, stood up and told the performers, "Now it's time for us to entertain you."

"Us?" Vanessa asked. "Which us?"

"Us us," I replied. "I want each of you to get out your paper bags." As Jessi passed out the Magic Markers, I told my brothers and sisters to draw a picture of their favourite animal on the bottom of the bag.

"But what are we going to do?" Adam asked.

I had already drawn the face of a cow on my bag. I slipped my hand in the bag and made the mouth move. "A puppet show!"

"Can we play, too?" the other kids asked.

"Of course." I had remembered to bring spare bags, and I passed them round.

The children stretched out on the lawn and laboriously worked on their drawings. When they had finished, Jessi said, "We need a stage. The toolshed would be perfect!"

"Great," I agreed. "And let's do a song, like *Old Macdonald*, so we can introduce each animal. Now we need an orchestra. Everybody, grab your instrument out of your rucksack."

Jessi and I put together the craziest orchestra ever. Nicky and Margo had packed matching kazoos, Vanessa had brought a plastic harmonica, and Claire had found a little toy trumpet. Jordan had a slide whistle, while Adam crashed together a pair of cymbals made out of two aluminium flan cases. But Byron's instrument was the cleverest of all—a tuba made from a piece of garden hose and a funnel.

The puppet show worked out better than we could ever have imagined. Nicky started it off, crouching behind the toolshed, his lizard puppet held in the air, while the band blasted out *Old Macdonald*. He sang the first verse of the old rhyme, then was joined by several turtles, a lion, a giraffe, two bears, and a brontosaurus. The kids tried to crouch behind the little toolshed but they got so crowded that they finally stood in a row in front of it.

"It's better like this," Jessi murmured to me, as the kids worked the mouths of their animals while singing the song or playing their instruments. "Now they can see each other's puppets and perform at the same time."

When all the animals had been introduced, and had had their chance to dance back and forth, the song came to an end.

"That was great," Suzi Barrett said. "What should we do next?"

"We'd love to stay," I said, "but the Explorers have a lot more things to do today."

"There's more?" Margo asked. "I can't believe it."

"Why not?" Jessi asked, kneeling in front of her to retie her tennis shoelace.

"This was so much fun, I thought our day was over."

"No way!" I laughed. "We've only just begun." I blew shrilly on my whistle and shouted, "Follow me, Explorers!"

Jessi and I led the parade out of the garden. Each of the kids now carried a puppet on his or her hand and wore an Explorer hat.

Next stop was the playground or, as Jessi and I had renamed it for the day, the Secret Garden.

"Why secret?" Margo asked, pushing her newspaper hat back on her head.

"Because there are secret clues hidden all over this playground—I mean, garden," I explained.

"And you have to find them," Jessi added.

"Clues?" Nicky's eyes were two huge blue circles. "Really?"

Jessi nodded. "You see, there is a hidden treasure here in the Secret Garden."

"And you have to follow the clues to find it," I said.

"Where do we start?" Vanessa asked. She was just as intrigued by the idea of a treasure hunt as her younger brothers and sisters.

I took off my newspaper hat, unfolded it, and found (where I had written it the night before) the first clue:

Welcome, Explorers, to the hunt for treasure.
We hope you find this event a pleasure.
Your next clue is where people eat (if they're able).
It's a piece of furniture. We call it a ...

"Table!" the kids shouted in unison. Jessi and I stood back and watched my brothers and sisters run from picnic table to picnic table, searching for the next clue.

"Going out at seven in the morning to hide these wasn't exactly my idea of a good time," I murmured to Jessi, "but watching those guys have fun makes it worth it."

"I found it!" Vanessa yelled, pulling off the piece of paper I'd taped under one of the tables. She waved it in the air, and the other kids clustered around to hear her and read it out loud. For a second they stood, thinking,

149

and then Jordan shouted, "I know where it is."

"Where is the next clue?" Jessi whispered to me.

"In the dustbin."

For the next fifteen minutes, the kids raced from the table to the dustbin, then to the swing set, on to the big maple tree, and over to the log bench with the name Barbie carved on its side.

What was truly amazing was that they were helping each other solve the puzzle. Claire and Margo held hands while Nicky and the triplets, who managed to be the first to arrive at every clue, would eagerly hand the piece of paper to Vanessa to read. Sometimes Vanessa let Claire unfold it. Other times Nicky would shout, "Please, let me!" But not once did they get into an argument. They were working together. Like a family.

It's hard to describe the warm feeling that kept bubbling up inside me. Not for the first time that day, tears welled in my eyes. (I think I'm turning into a big mush, just like Mary Anne.)

Suddenly Jordan called, "I've got it!" He picked up Claire and stumbled towards the sandpit next to the slide.

The other kids followed and knelt in the grass around the sandpit, where Jessi and I had buried the treasure. Jordan stuck his hand into the sand and pulled out a brightly coloured box. Then the rest of them dived in and started pulling prizes out of the sand.

"Look!" Nicky declared, holding up a little box with his name on it. "This one's for me."

Jessi had had the fantastic idea to take Animal Crackers boxes, paint them, and put each kid's name on one of them. Then we filled the boxes with cookies, wiggly plastic spiders and snakes, and wind-up toys.

The next half hour was spent eating treats at the picnic tables and examining the kids' treasures.

"This is the best day ever!" Claire declared.

And it was. Everything went off without a hitch. Soon the kids packed their treasures into their rucksacks, and then Jessi and I and my brothers and sisters went out for burgers and chips. Along the way, the Explorers stopped to watch some squirrels playing in the park and to feed the ducks in the pond. Then we saw the ice cream van and I treated everyone to Popsicles.

When our special day came to an end, Jessi and I led a very contented but tired band of Explorers back to the house. The sun was just starting to set, and the sky had turned a glowing shade of pink. We sat on the front steps and watched the sun sink below the horizon. Claire was sitting on my lap, and Nicky and Margo were leaning against my knee. The triplets surrounded

Jessi, and Vanessa sat between us. At that moment, I realized I could never give up babysitting, or being with children. I like them too much.

Besides, they're wonderful material for stories. And it just so happens that in my creative writing class on Friday, Mr Dougherty asked us to come up with a story about a special, unforgettable event. I know what mine is going to be about.

# THE BABYSITTERS CLUB MYSTERIES

Our favourite Babysitters are super-sleuths too! Don't miss the new series of Babysitters Club Mysteries:

Mysteries coming soon:

## No 1: Stacey and the Missing Ring
When Stacey's accused of stealing a valuable ring from a new family she's been sitting for, she's devastated – Stacey is *not* a thief! One way or another the Babysitters have *got* to find that ring and save the reputation of the Club . . . before it's too late!

## No 2: Beware, Dawn!
Just *who* is the mysterious "Mr X" who's been sending threatening notes to Dawn and phoning her while she's babysitting, *alone*? Dawn is determined to get to the bottom of this mystery, but she's *pretty* scared . . . what if she's in real danger?

*Look out for:*

**No 3: Mallory and the Ghost Cat**
**No 4: Kristy and the Missing Child**
**No 5: Mary Anne and the Secret in the Attic**
**No 6: The Mystery at Claudia's House**